ROAD TO SOUL

by Carmen Mendoza

First Printing, 2014   BellaSpark Press
www.BellaSpark.com

ISBN: 978-0-9899335-3-7
Cover design by: Kerrie Flanagan
Cover Photo by Carmen Mendoza

Credits
Chapter Photos: Cover, Mojave Nights, Selkie Desert, Desert Gator,
and A New Beginning by Carmen Mendoza
Flash Flood: Greg Mendoza
Original Artwork
Bar Fly and Seeds: Edwin Bomgardner

Endorsements

"After reading many technical journals and manuals on a daily basis I enjoy a good story for my evening reading. Carmen's stories hit the mark for enjoyable reading. I love the southwest flavor and cleaver twists to the stories"
A. R. Bonanno, Ed.D, psychologist

"…creative, thoughtful and very intriguing. Carmen shows great imagination in her stories, she captured my attention and I didn't want to stop reading…"
Betty Aragon-Mitotes, community leader and advocate

"…sassy and has sizzle"
Louise Creager, Realtor Extraordinaire and local speaker

"Intrigue. Adventure. Self-reflection. The latest creation from Carmen Mendoza weaves a fun yet thought-provoking adventure that invites us in and challenges us to explore our own fears and motivations…"
Deberah Bringleson, International Speaker and Author

Acknowledgements

No project is ever created or completed by one person. Somewhere along the path to the finish, an individual or group of people helped in some way to make it all come together. It is no different with this fictional writing.

Thank you to those friends—Ruth Klassen, Mary Breen, Shae Lee, Sonia Cooper, Judy Edwards and Penny Finuf—with whom in the beginning I dared to share my writings. Thank you for listening to me read my stories, or parts of the stories, to you. You all gave me encouragement to continue.

Thank you, my dear precious friend Joan King, for always believing in me and encouraging me to let these writings see the light by having them published.

Thank you so much Bill Greenleaf, my editor who, from the very first, understood the fear I had of sharing my writings with a professional and gave me encouragement to continue writing more than just this project.

My friend Donna Visocky, of *BellaSpark Magazine*, thank you for offering to publish my book and for helping me in the formatting of the hard copy.

And finally to Kerrie Flanagan, Director of Northern Colorado Writers, for helping me out in a pinch when I became frustrated with how to work the computer editing program and for your assistance in the final layout.

Dedication

I dedicate this fiction to my high school English teacher Mr. Ernest Crutcher. The creative writing seed took deep root in the soil of your teaching in high school. It lay dormant over forty years before breaking through the soil, reaching toward the sun with joy. I wonder if you were the voice coming from the other side of the veil that day in January 2009.

Table of Contents

Preface

One cold January day in 2009, I was in the kitchen washing dishes by hand and looking out at the snow-covered backyard when a bodiless voice clearly spoke to me from my left side: ". . . and then it happened. Between mile marker 165 and 164, the road disappeared."

The moment I heard the crystal-clear statement, I thought what an interesting story it would make. The statement kept showing up in my thoughts for the next six weeks, till I sat down one mid-morning at the end of February and let it pour out of me and onto the screen of my computer.

Three hours of writing felt like fifteen minutes. Within that time, I had written thirteen pages of a story that I titled Mojave Nights. Over the next four years, other stories started to emerge from the recesses of my mind to be put on paper. Each one tells its own story, intertwining with each other, all taking place from an isolated road in the desert of Southern California.

Please enjoy these stories as you travel on a very sacred road in the Mojave Desert I call Road To Soul.

~Carmen

Chapter 1
Mojave Nights

It was a new-moon night. No light. Not even a sliver. Never-ending blackness stretched in all directions. The faint night breeze barely rustled. The only light shining on the desert floor came from the vast bright stars hovering over the landscape.

She could see the beginnings of Scorpio forming in the east. If she looked to the north, she could make out the Seven Sisters, the Pleiades, which were seen best when one did not look straight at them. On a new-moon night, they came out of hiding and danced for anyone who took time to search for them.

Driving the two-lane highway, guided only by the car lights, she felt as if she was the only human alive on this stark, dark planet. She was relaxed from the two Vicodin® she had taken just before getting off the plane. Yet her senses were keen. She had traveled this road many times, both day and night, and the feeling was always the same: lonely, yet alive.

She used the center white line as a guide for driving to guarantee she would not get too close to the right edge of the road and have the sand reach up, grab her tire, and flip her car end over end. Many people had died out here that way, not to be found for hours or days after it happened. Dead Man's Road, they called it. No other cars would likely pass, and cell phone service didn't exist to call for help.

Not many people took this particular road, choosing instead to go a bit farther down the freeway and then travel on a more popular road, even though it meant another hour before arriving at their destination. Even her brother, the mechanic, would not drive this road. But she did. She enjoyed the solitude and the fresh, crisp night air the high desert emitted.

The light from the multitude of stars gave a silver-gray tone to the desert, creating monsters from the shapes of the Joshua trees that grew in abundance throughout the area. She shivered, gazing at their shapes as she whizzed by in her rental car.

Yet with all of this, she felt at home, at peace, able to breathe, rest, relax, and let down her guard. Here she had no one to watch out for, to hide from, or pretend with. Here, on this road, she was free to be her wild, gypsy made-up self who said and did what she wanted without worry about what people would say about her. She was free, and it was liberating and frightening all at once.

She shivered again. A smile came across her face, and she relaxed into the feeling of being completely alive and alone in a place of few people.

And then it happened. Between mile marker 165 and 164, the road disappeared. A flash of light, off to the left, appeared in a dark valley between two even darker mountains. At the same time she saw the light flash, she felt a powerful vibration pulsate through her entire being down to the core of her cells. She jammed on her brakes, laying skid marks in the middle of the road, practically turning the car sideways. Breathing heavily and choking on the brake fumes, she realized she had stopped not from the light but from what it had done to her.

"What the hell?" She caught her breath, and her racing heart struggled to escape from her chest. Such an intense wave of energy had penetrated her that she was dizzy from its effects. As her heart started to calm down, she could almost breathe

3

normally again.

She thought she faintly heard in the distance drumming and stomping on the soft earth. Had she gone crazy? Those damn painkillers were starting to give her hallucinations. She knew she needed to lay off taking so many of them, and now they were beginning to affect her mind. Shit!

As her ears adjusted to the sound, she realized she *was* hearing drumming, and it was coming from the distant glow of light in the valley to her left. She rationalized that some two-legged desert rat was having a party. She shook off the scared feeling that there were people near, focused on the road ahead, and prepared to continue her travel . . .

Where the hell was the road? She saw only dust in the beams of her car's headlights. She knew she had not gone off the side of the road because she was still upright, and as fast as she had been driving before all this crazy stuff happened, by all accounts, her car should have its wheels up with her trapped underneath. Instead her car was upright. There was just no freaking road. Where the hell had it gone?

Damn! What the fu . . .? She closed her eyes, took a deep breath, and called forth a calm to move into her body and mind. She took a couple more deep breaths, holding them and then letting them out, relaxing her entire body. She opened her eyes. Still, no road. She struggled to get out of the car, her body tense and sore from being in one position for so long. She took time

4

to gingerly stand upright. Once that was accomplished, she walked slowly around the car. As if her car had been picked up off the road and placed in the desert, she saw no tire tracks. She looked beyond the car as far as the lights would allow. No road anywhere. It was totally gone.

As much as she wanted to walk beyond the car and explore where the road had gone, she was acquainted enough with the desert to know to stay with the car. She knew not to go wandering off into the desert unless she wanted to end up as bleached bones and become one with the desert.

Stay in the car till morning, she told herself. She had her bowie knife, which she had gotten from the Alamo at Christmas while visiting dear friends in Texas. She had her below-zero weather coat, water, and food. *Make a bed in the backseat. Cuddle up with the bowie and wait it out.*

As the night grew darker, with her hunched down on the backseat below the windows, she thought of her life back in Denver. Divorced with a grown daughter she never saw, she worked long hours from her home office in her townhome in Highlands Ranch with only a neutered cat and chronic pain to keep her company. God, how she hated her life. So drab. No spark, no boyfriend, not even a "wham bam thank you ma'am" from time to time.

She could only blame herself; it was her own fault. She never went anywhere anymore, and because of that, people eventually stopped calling her and inviting her to parties and other events. Her only adventure was taking this very trip from time to time to hang with her siblings and a drunk in a little washed-up desert town out in the middle of nowhere. The drive of the foreboding road was the highlight of these trips, and here she was, for the first time ever, stuck.

The bowie brought little comfort. She liked to think she was skilled with knives, but she knew that would be lying. All she could do was thrust the knife forward and hope it hit its mark. She wished now that she had actually taken some lessons.

She settled down with the thought that the desert had always been her friend. She remembered feeling safe camping with her ex-husband only when they were in total isolation. She remembered the times she worked as a ranger in the National Park Service, taking city people on campouts and feeling smug that she felt at home in the wild as they struggled to come to terms with the unfamiliar. So she called upon those feelings and called out in her mind to have Mother Earth protect her as the night passed. With that, she fell asleep from sheer exhaustion and a little extra help from some little white friends she kept in the medicine bottle on her person at all times.

Hours later, as the new morning light gently made its debut and danced across the valleys, gullies, hills, mountains, and Joshua trees, she slept deeply. Little did she realize she would

6

not be alone much longer. Out of the desert, from the direction that the light and sounds had come from the night before, a group of people slowly came toward her. They had seen the sun bounce off the metal of her car from where they camped for the night and came to inspect it.

About thirty of them of all ages—men, women, and children—walked silently toward her, spread out. Neither they nor the dogs that traveled with them emitted a sound, and she was not aware they were coming closer.

She woke up with the soft morning light bathing the backseat and crawled out of the car slowly, looking down at the ground as she emerged. They came closer, unnoticed. She stretched and flexed her body, still looking at the ground as she walked away from the car, searching for the nonexistent road. She heard a snap and looked up just in time to see the group close the ten-yard gap between them and her. She froze, and her breath caught.

A tall, middle-aged man moved forward, separating himself from the rest of the group. The moment she saw him, his reflective raven-black eyes captured her with such force that she found herself stepping backward till she was blocked by the body of her car. He was two inches taller than she was and had shiny, loose black hair to his waist with hints of gray sprinkled through it. He was intimidating and exciting all at once. She forgot there were other people with him as he stopped inches in front of her. He loomed over her.

Her heart pounded in her ears. What the hell was happening? Where did these people come from? Who were these people? She dared to take her eyes off his and glanced over his shoulder at the group. They looked like they'd stepped out of one of her books on desert dwellers she had at home. She noticed both men and some women were bare-chested. The children were naked. Some of the older people had geometric patterned tattoos on their torsos. They surrounded her, along with the man who was still very much too close to her.

She did not realize she still held the knife till he swiftly grabbed her wrist and squeezed so hard her fingers popped open. The knife fell easily from her hand to the ground. He let go of her wrist and stepped back. He picked up the knife and stared at it, then looked back to her with puzzled surprise.

~~~~

Such a big knife for someone who seemed not to know how to use it, he thought. Such a strange person she seemed. He focused on the woman. She was a woman. Yes, he could tell she had breasts as his eyes took in her curves under the covering she wore. What was she wearing? He had never seen anything like her or her clothing. She was covered in colorful cloth and had funny coverings on her feet. He came closer to inspect her, taking her in from head to toe with his gaze.

Her green-brown eyes were wide with fear, and she backed

up as he inspected her. Her graying hair was cut at her shoulders. He could smell the sweet scent she gave off. A longing stirred in his loins, and he found himself intrigued.

What was that thing she was leaning on? He had watched her crawl out of it as his group had approached her. He had never seen anything like it. He walked around the car looking into the windows, carefully touching the chrome, feeling the metal cooled from the night's cold. He stooped to look at the wheels, reaching to touch the tires. He shook his head, not understanding.

A considerably older woman approached him from the group. The elder explained that this was a woman from another time. Breathmaker had brought her here to them for a reason. They were to take her into their group and allow her to become one of them. She was a gift. He did not understand, but the old woman's eyes danced softly as she reached up and patted his cheeks with her wrinkled, sun-browned hands. She expected him to accept this strange event without question. The old woman turned and looked at the alien woman. As she passed the stranger, she smiled and said, "Welcome," though the newcomer did not understand.

He turned and faced the strange woman from another time, motioning that she was to follow him. Them. She did not understand what he was telling her. He grabbed at her wrist, but she jumped back, and he grabbed air. This made him angry. He turned and called on two young men in the group.

~~~~

The men approached her. One of them produced a yucca rope from a pouch at his waist. Both grabbed her by the waist and arms. Before she could move, they jerked her hands together and one of them quickly wrapped her hands in front of her with the rope. He held the remaining end of the rope and pulled her forward, her hands bound tight. The other young man walked beside her.

She felt like a dog on a leash as she was led into the desert away from her car, her belongings, her life, her very existence. She panicked. Fear and anger welled up inside of her at being treated without regard to her feelings. To her surprise, the anger brought courage. She dug her feet into the soft desert sand. She jerked hard on the rope. The one holding the end of the rope stopped, turned around, and only laughed as he tightened the distance between them and pulled her forward. She had to lunge and hop-skip to keep from falling face forward. The second young man did not help her but stayed by her side.

As she walked with her head down, barely seeing where she was going from the tears welling up in her eyes, she did all she could to understand her situation. After a time, she gathered the courage to look up and take in her surroundings. Where was the man with the obsidian eyes? Who was he? What had he and the old woman said to her? Who were these people, and where did they come from?

She scanned her surroundings and realized they were walking back toward where she had seen the light the night before. They did not walk in a single line, but spread out, with children and dogs running between the adults. Several children ran along beside her. Some became brave enough to touch her. They squealed and ran off, only to run back and do it again. It somewhat annoyed her, but she was in no position to protest.

She finally saw the man who seemed to be in charge of her destiny. She decided to focus on him. He was in the middle of the group toward the front. It was apparent he was leading them. Was he some sort of chief or medicine man or what? She watched as he walked. Pausing, he took in the whole panorama in front of him. With his head lifted to the sky, he closed his eyes and breathed deeply of the air. The group stopped, waiting for him to continue. He opened his eyes and changed his direction slightly, and they followed.

On and on they walked till midday. She was amazed she could keep up. Or had they slowed their pace for her? She didn't know or care. She was tired, hungry, and in pain. Damn, all her belongings were back in the car. She had nothing to take even if they would let her.

Just as she felt she was going to succumb to the noonday heat, the group stopped by a huge clump of Joshua trees next to some large boulders. *Oh God, have mercy—shade!* she thought as she fell to the cool, sandy earth.

The young man who had walked beside her since they had tied her hands and dragged her from all she knew handed her a pouch full of water. She gratefully accepted it, and later would learn that the pouch was a deer bladder. She was so thirsty. She would have drunk all the sweet-tasting water if he had not ripped it out of her hands. He gave her a sour look, took a drink of water himself, and handed the pouch to the nearest person, who did the same.

People rested against the cool rocks or stretched out on the cool sand in the wash. She relaxed, knowing it was no use to try to get away. Her hands were still tethered to the guy at the other end of the rope. Besides, she was so tired from all the walking that she had no energy to try to escape. Before she knew it, she was asleep along with the others, while some of the men squatted on boulders keeping watch over the resting group.

She had just fallen asleep when she was catapulted to her feet, pulled forward, and marched on into the desert. Yet, she knew it had to have been longer than just seconds in the wash. She could tell some time had gone by as the sun sat lower on the horizon.

They walked on, gradually heading northeast. Days went by. A routine set in that she began to understand. Walk in the cooler part of the day, rest at high noon. Walk some more. Rest when you no longer could see the person in front of you. Get up and repeat again.

Days and days went by with this routine, only to be interrupted by small groups of men leaving to hunt from time to time. The people did not wait for them, and it amazed her that the hunters always found where the group was. They brought back rabbits, ground squirrels, and occasionally a deer. Women would gather the fruit, berries, or nuts of the plants they passed. This was what made up their diet. At least it was food. She wasn't starving.

She must have gone back in time. How and why? She had pondered that often as her feet raked over the desert floor. She must be back in time. Just look at their clothes, their tools, and the fact they had yet to come across a vehicle or roads or even see the train tracks that ran along the no-longer-existing road. She even looked and listened for planes in the sky, but all she ever saw was clouds, birds, and vast blueness. She had to be back in time, but how far? She had no idea. And worse, she had no idea how to get back to her time.

She must be dreaming. *But probably not,* she thought as she stubbed her toe on a rock hidden by the sand. The pain was real, so this must be real also.

As time went on, she had been able to study the individuals who made up the band. There was the old woman who first greeted her. Her skin was tattooed, wrinkled, and leathered, and she walked with a slight hunch. She seemed to be as old as the sand they walked on, yet her cobalt-blue eyes sparkled like fairy dust. Everyone in the band seemed to love her and value her opinion.

Then there were the two young men who had tied her hands when they first dragged her into the desert with them. They appeared to be very good friends, as they hunted together and ate together many times. They were full of spirit and enjoyed playing tricks on members of the group and making everyone laugh.

One of them seemed to be married, as she had noticed similarities to other couples. The pairs, both men and women, had scars of two deep cut marks about two inches long and a half inch apart across the top of their wrists, hers on the right and his on the left. Plus, the married women wore a choker necklace with a small pouch around their neck. One of the young men had those marks, and his wife seemed to be the sister or at least a relative of the other young man.

There were also young families, and she was amazed at how the mother and father both cared equally for the infant or child. One very shy young woman, very much in the latter stages of pregnancy, was attended to by just about everyone in the band. As her belly grew bigger, her husband never strayed too far from her side. Various people carried her bundle, and at night someone always rubbed her feet and back. Everyone seemed to own her belly, coming up and putting an ear to her stomach without permission. This did not bother the young woman, who seemed to relish the attention.

One very hot day, the young woman seemed to struggle to move forward with the group, stopping every now and then to stretch and to kneed her lower back. Shortly before noon, she let out a sharp yell and fell to her knees in pain. The ground was soaked with moisture, and excitement rippled throughout the group. A baby was coming.

Women hurried to her side and helped her to a place on the ground, while a group of men searched for a soft spot in the earth. Once they found one, they dug quickly as children brought soft mats to line the pit. A couple of women helped the young mother-to-be to the pit and tended to her, while another kept watch for the emergence of the baby. Her husband sat nearby, out of the way but watching, and his best friend sat with him. The other men formed a loose circle around the birthing mother and her attendants, some of the men facing in and others facing out, but all keeping watch. The whole tribe waited as a new member struggled to make his or her way into the world and into their lives. After what seemed to be hours, a new baby girl emerged. She and her mother were both wrapped in soft furs. The new father came and sat by his wife's side and held his new daughter for a very long time as each member of the band paid their respects and the new mother slept.

In the distance, the medicine man beat a drum and sang a song of welcoming and thanks for the newest member of the band. A girl was such a good blessing. The whole tribe rejoiced in this birth as much as they would the birth of a boy. They saw both sexes as equal—each offering to the other what they did not have—thus making them complete human beings.

That night the whole band formed a protective circle around the new family and slept. Having taken in the entire process from a distance, not wanting to get in the way and really not knowing what to do, she thought of her world and how babies were born, some in hospitals and some at home with midwives, but never with the whole community or extended family participating like she had just witnessed. She remembered her own lonely pregnancy and delivery. She had been ignored by her husband, merely tolerated. Tears flooded her eyes as she took on a new warm feeling for the people she was traveling with.

She felt someone watching her and looked up to see the guide taking in her every detail. She quickly looked away. He seemed to be always watching her with this detached yet inquisitive look, and it made her nervous, as she had been thinking, *What if he had been my daughter's father? How would he have treated her, taken care of her, loved her?* She quickly covered herself with her blankets and did her best to sleep.

Over the months she had been with these people, he had taken it upon himself to be her protector, companion, and jailer. She was never out of his sight, even when she was allowed to go for water. She could feel those obsidian eyes following her every move. From what she could tell of him, he was near her age, respected by the group, quiet, and had an uncanny way of guiding them around danger.

As the days and nights progressed, she found when they prepared for sleep each evening, he spread his mat closer and closer to hers. Even though it had been months, she never got over the feeling of excitement and fear when he was near, and it perplexed her. Slowly over time, he had closed the gap between them when the band bedded for the night. The last few nights, he had placed his mat near hers and slept with his head at her feet.

She could feel the season changing in the air. There were more clouds in the cobalt sky, and the nights were getting longer and colder. She was grateful for him lying beside her. He had such warmth emitting from his body that, once she calmed her fear, eventually she was able to fall asleep. He never touched her but lay by her, offering his comfort and protection.

This night was different. He had been looking at her more today than ever before. When he brushed close by her, he reached out and lightly touched her as he went to talk to an elder. His touch sent electricity throughout her entire body. As he passed, she looked up from the skin she was cleaning and watched his back, only to see him stop, turn, and stare at her. Her heart raced, and she felt warmth between her legs.

After a moment of taking her in with his eyes, he turned back, but she could not. She watched this man in his fifties, strong, walking erect with such confidence, move farther away from her. Transfixed, she focused on the sway of his long, shiny hair as he walked toward his destination. She shivered, looked down, and went back to work. This she remembered as she prepared for the night.

Silently, he came out of nowhere, picked up her mat, and moved it a distance from the group. He laid her mat down, overlapped his mat on hers, and placed a rabbit fur blanket on top. She started to shake. She did all she could not to let it show as she walked to him. What was going on? She did her best not to look at him. He lay down on the mat, under the blanket, and motioned for her to come beside him. He held the blanket open for her.

She looked down at him and gasped. He was not wearing anything. She dared look at his manhood. He was huge, thick, and uncircumcised. And very much waiting for her.

She slowly lowered her body, squatting down on her knees, then lay down with her back to him. She looked out at the stars and the distant shadow of the mountains, and her heart skipped a beat as she felt his warm hand on her waist. Just that one simple touch set her on fire, and she jerked as he rolled her onto her back toward him.

~~~~

The People of the Sand had seen him move her mat and knew what was coming. They went about their night business, acting as if they did not know what was about to take place. Eventually they heard lovemaking on the wind. The people were happy. He had been alone for such a long time, and she seemed to be a good match for him.

~~~~

She closed her eyes as he slid his hand up her sack-shaped dress and took it off over her head. Her modern clothes had fallen apart months ago, not able to hold up to the harsh desert wind and sun. He said something in his language. She did not open her eyes, and again he spoke the same words. She opened her eyes to see him staring at her. A small smile crossed his face as he gently took his middle finger and thumb and touched the outside of her right eye, as if to tell her to keep her eyes open and look at him.

As he did this, he slid silently and strongly on top of her. God, he felt so good. He took in her scent, deeply smelling her neck. His hand slipped under her head as he brought his lips to her cheek, neck, chest, and back up to her lips. The aroma of his yucca-washed hair filled her every pore, and she allowed herself to be caught in the net of his mane. As he kissed her inviting lips, he spread her legs apart with his knee and slid into her with ease. Her body arched up to meet his, accepting him as if she had known him all her life. Her mind fought to stay in control. It was as if across time, Creator had made their bodies for each other. They fit so well.

She did not realize she had closed her eyes till he spoke again. She was forced to look at him, in his eyes, as he drove deeper into her with his shaft. She had never felt this intense pressure of pleasure before. His eyes were engulfing her, and with each thrust of his body, she felt her body start to surrender as never before. She felt total abandonment, total surrender, as he pushed deeper and deeper into her. The reflections of the stars in his eyes grew brighter. She found herself shuddering in waves of release that overtook her entire body, and eventually she collapsed in a swell of cold sweat as her quivering body melted around him.

Never before with any man—and she had been with many—had she ever so deeply surrendered, totally letting go of control as she climaxed. A second later, he gave a primordial grunt, and she was filled with immense warm liquid to her core. He fell on her, panting, and she accepted his weight as she brushed his hair out of her face. After a while, still strong in her, he looked up at her and smiled. He cradled her in his arms. Within minutes they both were asleep, their bodies intertwined in the aftermath of fulfilling their desires.

Little did each of them know that Breathmaker had brought them together across time to share this life, to fill their lonely nights, and to bring comfort to each other as they grew old.

Each night after their first physical connection, they slept close together, sometimes wrapped within and around each other, intertwined like a Celtic knot. Every now and then, there had been a repeat performance of the first time he had made love to her. He did not need Viagra™ as so many men of her time seemed to need. She found she was physically satisfied as never before, and she slept with deep renewal.

Yet with all that intimacy and physical contact, she did not feel totally comfortable with him. They were not able to communicate verbally, and sometimes it was frustrating. He still made her nervous whenever he was near her, and she could not totally relax. Her feelings perplexed her.

They had been traveling for about eight months from what she could gather. The days were getting shorter and the nights longer. Would they ever stop wandering around in the desert? Would they ever stay in one place for more than a few nights? Would she ever get back to her time?

Late one evening just before dusk, young scouts came running into camp, excited. They had found tracks of a small herd of deer. The people had not eaten meat recently, and the group was elated in anticipation of venison. The young scouts reported to the guide the general direction of the herd. In no time, the men were prepared for the hunt. Bows, arrows, and spears accompanied every man as he left the camp and followed the ones who had found the deer.

It was left up to the women to follow, bringing up the rear of the human train with all the group's worldly possessions. The scene of getting ready reminded her of the movie *Dances with Wolves,* where the tribe prepared for the great buffalo hunt. She had seen the movie many times, never tiring of it. She must be in the past.

Once the tribe gathered, the older men skinned the deer after the leader had given a blessing for the life of the deer and the food and clothing it would provide for the people. The hunter who had made the first throw for the kill was given the heart. The women related to the hunter cleaned the hide, while other women carved the carcass, and still others made a fire to cook the first meal of meat in a long time. The tribe was happy, and she found herself smiling and drooling in anticipation of the feast to come. She looked up in time to see the guide chuckle at her eagerness.

For a while now, she and the guide had been together as a couple. She was enjoying getting to know him, his culture, and even his language. She was learning his faster than he was hers, which only made sense. She heard his language every day from many people who talked among themselves and to her. The sound was so beautiful, and she never tired of listening to it. On the other hand, he heard her language only when she spoke it for him. They would laugh at each other's attempt to make the sounds of the words from their respective languages.

Their laughter did not go unnoticed. The People of the Sand were deeply happy for them.

One early summer morning, she turned around slowly, taking in the beauty. Just before the last star of the night hid from the light of day and before the people rose, he had nudged her to wake up. She stretched and snuggled deeper into the covers. He poked his finger in her side, laughing at how she looked like a small child hiding in her mother's robes, and motioned for her to get up. She stretched again, cleared her eyes, and watched him prepare for the day knowing that this day was going to be different. They had not been up this early before, nor had he ever nudged her awake, always allowing her to wake with the rest of the band.

She saw he had his atlatl spear, his small bow and arrows, a water pouch, and a second pouch containing food. He handed her the food, keeping the weapons and water with him. She realized they, just the two of them, were going somewhere. She took the pouch and balanced it on her head as she had been taught by the women of the group. He handed her the bundle he had put together of the items the people had brought to them over the last few days. She took it and followed him into the desert.

She reflected on what the people had given them, which was in that bundle. A dress, a pouch given to him by the medicine man, a loincloth, and other things she did not understand. She realized as she walked behind him that the people knew they were leaving, but what was going on? Her heart skipped a beat as she followed him out into the desert, once again leaving something she had come to view as home and security.

She walked behind him for some distance till he paused, waiting for her to catch up. When she did, he continued on. She was surprised by this action. Usually women walked a foot back and to the side of the men they were with, not beside them unless they were equal in status. And she and this man were walking side by side. This simple action told her how important she was to him, and she felt like she was the queen of England. She was his equal.

At noon, they stopped to rest in the shade on the north side of some boulders and ate some of the food he had packed for them. He handed her the bladder of water, and she took just a swig, having learned the first day she had been with the people to be conservative with the water.

She thought back to that long-ago time and smiled. Her life was so different now. She had learned so much from the people: how to gather berries and seeds, as well as what plants were edible, and even how to skin a rabbit.

~~~~

He looked up from where he sat and caught her smile. He never tired of watching her. Everything about her fascinated him: the way she pulled her hair up out of her face, the way she tilted her head to the sun for moments at a time, the way she spoke in her language, the way she moved as she worked an animal skin with that odd knife of hers, and even the way she smiled. The effect she had on him was intoxicating, and he had never felt so alive.

Ever since the first time he had gathered the courage to take her and fill her with his maleness, he had thought of pulling her away from the people to be alone with him so he could do what he wanted with her without an audience. The thought of what he was going to do to her made him smile, and he could not wait till they arrived at their destination, where he planned to make her totally and utterly his. His woman. His mate.

~~~~

After resting a bit, they continued their journey. He spoke to her from time to time, explaining the landscape, teaching her how to detect water and read tracks in the sand. She enjoyed the attention he was giving her, and she enjoyed watching his muscles stretch and grow taut as he bent down to the ground to point out bird tracks. She never tired of watching him, his red-brown body glistening in the desert afternoon sun.

She noticed that for some time they had been walking toward a small mountain in the western distance. The mountain jutted out of the desert floor and stood by itself. It was not like the mountains near Denver that she was used to. This mountain was made completely out of a pile of dark white and buff sandstone boulders, as if a giant had scooped up pebbles from another place and plopped them in a big pile in the middle of nowhere. She realized the small mountain of pebbles was not really small, for it seemed, though they walked toward the mountain, they never got closer to it. No wonder they had left so early in the morning. But why were they going here, and what would they find?

By midafternoon, they finally arrived at the pebble mountain. As they got closer, his pace quickened. He seemed excited, and she watched him as he raced twenty yards ahead of her. He walked right up to the nearest boulder and disappeared! She blinked her eyes. One moment he was in front of her, and the next he had vanished. She blinked again, and he was back in the same place she had seen him moments ago.

Had she been out in the sun too long? Was this a way back to her time? These thoughts were heavy on her mind as she closed the distance that had grown between them while walking.

She hurried closer to where he was waiting for her, and she

saw behind him streaks of various colors on the rocks with slits that were only visible if one was right in front of the two overlapping boulders. She looked at where he stood, and then suddenly her eyes got big, as she realized the boulders made the perfect outline of a woman's vagina, color and all. He laughed at her shock.

He excitedly took her hand and led her through the deepest slit in the formation. It was tight, and they had to wiggle to make their way through. After a few short yards, the boulders opened up to a dark, thick, green patch of grass. Lush, almost tropical plants of all types and a deep pool of cobalt-blue water spread out before them. This oasis was so beautiful. He delighted in her pleasure as he watched her jump up and down with joy, and he almost lost his balance when she unexpectedly jumped into his arms. He fell to the soft grassy ground with her on top of him, and they rolled around in the grass laughing like two little kids.

Eventually they stopped rolling. Their eyes locked, drawing each into the other, her into his onyx-rich eyes and him into her deep yellow-flecked, green-brown eyes. She became nervous again and quickly rolled off him. She turned her back to him, afraid he would see and feel her mixed emotions. Instead, she concentrated on taking in the beauty of this enchanted place.

She heard him get up, brush himself off, and move away

from her to the other side of the pond. She watched from where she stood. Standing in front of a little alcove, he glanced around at the ground, the sides of the surrounding boulders, the desert willow just off to the side, and the grass. He looked across the pond at her and smiled. She continued to watch as he walked in a sun-wise circle, patting down the tall grass with his feet as she had seen Grass Dancers do just before a powwow began, preparing the ground for the other dancers who were to follow.

She stood quietly with respect, watching this stunning man tamp the grass with his powerful legs and start to dance, twist and turn, dip and glide. His braided hair danced along with the rest of his body, as his feet patted down the soft, lush grass. He was beautiful to watch. She realized she was seeing something very ancient and felt privileged to witness this ritual.

Once he had completed his task, he stopped. Taking his little medicine bag from around his neck, he held it up to the west, where the sun hung in the sky. Then he turned to the north, east, and south, above and below, pausing at each direction for a moment. Finally, he brought it to his heart and said a short prayer. Then he put the necklace back on his bare chest, untangled his braids from the string, turned to face her, and motioned for her to come to him.

Her heart skipped a beat. She knew something very important was going to happen in this special Shangri-La place, and she was a part of it. She trembled as she slowly and carefully made her way around the pond to him, wondering what was going to happen.

She sat down on the matted grass and felt as if she were sitting on a plush bed at a Hilton. She started to say something to him, but he brought his finger to his lips, looking past her. In the reeds next to the pond scampered two plump desert rabbits. He moved ever so slowly, not making a sound, and reached for his bow and an arrow where he had laid them on a flat rock. He silently placed the small arrow on the bow and cocked the animal-gut string, and within a blink of an eye, one rabbit lay quivering but dead. Dinner. She stood up silently, gathering twigs and sticks from the area to start a fire. He took her knife and started to skin the still-warm, fat rabbit.

The stars were starting to come out as they finished a dinner of roasted pinion nuts and rabbit. She leaned back on her elbows, stretched out her legs toward the fire, and flexed her feet. Looking up at the gathering night sky, she had never felt so satisfied.

~~~~

He watched her out of the corner of his eye. He took in the length of her body and marveled at how she had changed from when he'd first met her. She was more toned, and he loved how dark her skin had gotten under the desert sun, almost as dark as the people, yet she was not one of them.

He observed her as she viewed the Milky Way, her eyes

soaking up the vast starlight from the millions and billions of stars that stretched in a band from horizon to horizon.

He noticed that faraway look she would get at times when she looked in the night sky or the horizon. He wished he could soothe the fear and loneliness he saw in her eyes when she would look out across the landscape. All he knew was to love her in his way, and that was what he had in mind on this trip— to make her his in every way possible. He wanted her to know that she was home and was one of the People of the Sand.

~~~~~

Remembering the first time she had seen the Milky Way, out in this very desert many years ago, and how it had grabbed her heart with such intensity, she clutched her chest and sobbed deeply. She looked up at the sky. She had no idea not seeing the Milky Way since leaving the desert over thirty years ago had had such an effect on her. The long years in the city had stripped her of her very life, and she had no idea how it had happened or when. Now she was in the very place she had often envisioned, fully content with her life, stretched out next to the most amazing man she had ever known.

~~~~~

He noticed the shift in her, and realizing she had returned to this time and place, he turned toward her, taking in her beauty. His eyes soaked up her hair, the shape of her face, her succulent lips, her still-perky breasts, her belly, and her strong, tan legs. He focused on every detail of her being, and she let him.

They both reached for each other, hungry for what each had to give to the other. Wrapped in each other's arms, they fell gently to the soft grassy mat, kissing. Stroking with such need for the touch, feel, and smell of the opposite sex, they hurriedly pulled off what clothes they had on, stripping in seconds without ever breaking contact.

He climbed on her, putting his arms under her hips and raising her to him as she opened herself to receive him. They met with such force, such abandon, such rawness, with the need of a man and a woman so great that new stars formed in the sky from the deep impact they created. Sweat mingled as two of Breathmaker's people blended in the deepest, most intimate way possible to express the very existence of a Creator. The sweet smell they emitted with their combined essence permeated the magical oasis and added to the life of all that witnessed this union.

Panting together, they laughed as they clasped onto one another and caught their breath. Their pounding hearts eventually beat out a slower cadence, as each stroked the other's face. She laid her head on his chest, listening to his heart return to a resting beat as he stroked her back with one hand and covered them in the fur blanket with the other.

All that witnessed this union smiled at the two humans as

they slept in the magic of a place in the desert known to the people of the area as the Womb of Mother Earth.

The next morning, they woke to the sun high in the sky, and they giggled like two naughty children who had been caught oversleeping. They quickly ate the dried seed cakes they had brought with them and took their time bathing in the pond, feeling the warm, mineral-rich water wake their souls. Almost falling back to sleep, they let the sun dry their fully loved bodies.

He knew she was almost asleep again; however, they had things to do before the day was over, and he had to explain to her as best he could what they were. He splashed water on her warm body, and she jolted up with a sharp trill and splashed water back at him. After the short-lived water fight, they dried in the grass, and he tossed her clothes to her. She seemed to know that they were getting ready for something important.

He sat down near their sleeping mat and motioned for her to sit down opposite him. He had the bundle the people had given them before the two left on their trip. He carefully opened the bag and pulled out a small pouch. He set that aside. He pulled out the deer hide dress made for her by the elder women in the band. He handed her the dress, motioning for her to not open it, but to set it aside. He pulled out a loincloth and set it near him. He then picked up the smaller bag, carefully opened it, and took out the contents one by one. There were bags of yellow, black, white, and red clay, various fetishes, loose tobacco, and a clay pipe. These he set carefully in the middle of their sleeping mat. Then he sat back, looking at what he had placed before them. She waited. He was sitting on his knees with his hands on his thighs. After a bit, he looked up at her and hoped that she could see this was important to him. He needed her to listen and pay close attention.

He reached out, took her hands in his, and looked into her eyes. She met his coal-black gaze. He told her he loved her. She was the other half of his heart, and he had never felt as alive as when he was with her. Breathmaker had brought her across time just for him, and he wanted to make her all his, only his, to be his wife forever and always, if she would have him.

Her hands began to tremble in his, and her breaths quickened.

~~~~

Here it was, all she had ever wanted in a man, all she'd needed and wished for with each new relationship, only to be disappointed over and over again. Until now. Here he was, her dream, her desire, her mystical ever-elusive man, right before her eyes, and he was asking her to marry him. She realized this was what the light and vibration was all about, to bring her to this man, meant only for her. Her eyes moistened, and she nodded her head yes. He squeezed her hands and pulled her to him. He wrapped himself around her with such force that her breath was taken away.

~~~~

Certain that she understood, he then explained the purpose of each item: her dress, his loincloth, and the importance of each color. The ceremony they were to conduct together, witnessed by Breathmaker, and was to take place as the sun set in the west and the full moon came up in the east at the same time. But before that, they had much to do. He needed to hunt for their marriage meat, and she needed to grind the various seeds, corn, and grain that they had been given by the elders and make it into cakes. The preparation of the marriage bed had to be finished from what he had started the day before, and of course, they had to dress and decorate their bodies for each other.

~~~~

While he left the oasis to hunt, she busied herself with the preparation of the marriage ceremony and wedding night. She shook out the bedding, then repositioned and smoothed the skins.

From one of the pouches they had brought with them, she took out handfuls of seeds and started carefully grinding them on a flat rock she had found that would work as a metate. She used a rock that fit in the palm of her hand as a mano. As she ground the corn and seeds into a meal, she thought of so many things.

She remembered the many manos and matates she had seen in every cliff dwelling she had been to in the Southwest. She remembered grinding corn for tourists, and even that little demonstration was backbreaking. Yet here she was, in the best shape of her life, grinding corn in the same way women had done for eons, but this time it was not for demonstration but for her binding to the man of her soul. She took a deep, quickening breath, realizing that her life was really happening.

She also thought of her "modern" life and how lost, lonely, and out of place she had felt most of the time, even when she seemed content with all the modern conveniences she had surrounded herself with. She thought of all the people she had known in that time, and her heart ached for most of them, as she realized she would never see them again.

At the same time, she thought of the people she had come to know as her family and friends, and her heart warmed. She realized that life was a journey of experiences. People moved in and out of that journey, some staying for a while and others only minutes, but each had touched her and molded her into who she was today. She said a silent prayer. In her heart and mind, she released each person from her past life as she continued to grind the meal for the marriage dinner.

~~~~

One day, after she and her husband had returned to be with

the others, they came upon a horizon that looked somewhat familiar. No. It couldn't be. Turning around slowly, she took in the view. Yes. It was. Her heart pounded. A big smile came across her face. This was *her* beloved desert, the place she had put up with the drunk for. Maybe, just maybe, she could find a way home. But did she want to go home? Wasn't this now her home? She was a mated woman. The two scars on her right wrist indicated she was married. She was happy. But if she could go back, would she? And would he come with her? Home.

She stopped dead in her tracks. Home. The thought was exciting, yet she felt a tug deep in her heart. The people, over the many months, had slowly become her family. She had found someone to share her nights with. She couldn't leave. She couldn't stay. Could she?

The people noticed her excitement. She was able to communicate to them that she knew this place. She ran toward the outcropping of iron rocks. Could they be her rocks? Did she dare believe this was where she'd meditated often? She found the place where she'd fallen asleep on the smooth rock surface. In her own time, this place had made her feel connected to the ancient ones in the valley that stretched before her. Yes. It was her outcropping. The very place she spent hours looking to the valley below feeling a deep connection as the sun baked her skin.

But wait, something was different. The markings were the same, only there was a thin coating of desert varnish on them. Only last year, the petroglyphs were almost white. She knew it took eons for the rains and the rust to spread a thin coat of brown red over the rock to darken the marks. This just did not make sense.

No longer worried she would run from them, as she was now one of them, having been to the sacred place where all unions were blessed, the people watched her explore this place with abandon.

She stood up from the rocks, gathered her bearings, and for the first time noticed the ruins of a house on her right. What? Ruins? This could not be. The cabin she remembered was new, only a couple of years old. She slowly walked down the slope, her eyes taking in the shape of what was left of a cabin. There was no roof, but the shape of the house was correct. She stopped in front of what should be the front door and stared. There were the remains of a cinderblock porch but not much else. The sharp edges had been worn down by the sands of time. She sat down, head in her hands, and wept. How could this be? She was not in the past. She was in the future! What had happened? She remained in this position for a long time, lost. The people let her be.

Eventually she looked up, wiped the tears from her eyes, and gazed across the horizon to the valley that stretched in front of the cabin. She could see just a few yards away the faint outline of the garden and the outhouse to the right. Yes, there was no doubt. This was her magic place, and it was in ruins. *Oh, my God, what happens now?*

The people realized this was where she was from. They did not know or understand the shape of the ruins, but knew that people had lived there long ago. They had come upon many similar places over time in their wanderings of this area. They let her alone to be with her emotions.

She had never felt so alone, so lost, and so confused. It dawned on her that she had no idea where in time she was and that she had no understanding of why this was happening to her. She was so deep in thought that she did not hear him come up to her, but she felt gentle arms embrace her from behind.

~~~~~

She collapsed in his hold, and he tightened his grip to keep her from falling. He slowly lowered her to the ground, never letting go, as she sobbed from a place of such pain that his heart broke for her. He stroked her hair and spoke softly, reassuring her in his language that he would always be there for her and take care of her. She was his heart, his soul, his very existence, and he could never let her be hurt.

Did she understand all that he was saying? It did not matter. She was starting to quiet down, responding to his soothing words and gentle yet strong arms supporting and protecting her. He held on, slowly and softly stroking her hair, cooing to her till she no longer cried at all.

~~~~

Eventually she looked up, brushed the tears from her eyes, and reached up to kiss him deeply while hugging him. She was so blessed to have this man she had prayed for, searched for on dating websites, and waited for, for over twenty years. It was weird that she had to go forward in time to find him. Talk about cyberspace!

They stayed in her beloved valley for several days more than they had in other places. With water at the surface, lots of trees and shrubs, and plentiful animal life to feed off, they took advantage of the abundance Breathmaker had given this valley.

She had traveled with the people for a year now. Had twelve months passed since she drove between the mile markers in May of last year? The desert felt like it did the night she last was in a car. It was the beginning of summer from what she could tell from the sky and the position of the stars.

Over the year, she had grown used to their language, even learning a good part of it. It sounded like water gently trickling over smooth rocks. It was soothing to listen to the people talk as she fell asleep each night beneath the twinkling lights of the black sky, wrapped in the arms of a most sacred man. The sound of their language calmed her when her thoughts overtook her, when she felt like she was going to panic as she gave thought to her situation and what she should do.

She thought of her sisters and brothers, her daughter, and the people she knew back in Colorado and the backwater town she had been heading to. How long had they looked for her before they had forgotten her?

As she prepared for the night, she felt conflicted. She realized with some surprise that she was content to be where she was. She had lost weight, and her body had responded to the constant walking. She was tone, tan, flexible, and no longer hurting. Amazing! And she had found a companion, a lover, and a husband in the silent guide of the group. He was everything she had ever wanted in a life partner and more.

And yet she missed the people of her time. She missed her time. She missed the technology, the planes, TV, movies, restaurants, and showers. *Oh God, the showers and running hot water and . . .*

She stopped, stood up, and stared across the vast open desert at the familiar horizon, only to be distracted by a gentle hand reaching up and taking hers. She gracefully stooped to lie beside him.

She no longer needed to look for the opening to her world in the fabric of time. She was home. She realized deep in her soul, wherever he was, she was home in his strong, protective arms. She was content to lie on her back and allow his body heat to warm and protect her from the creeping cold blanket of the Mojave night. She watched Scorpio come up over the horizon as the sisters danced in the eastern summer night sky. She closed her eyes as her body merged with his and knew she was truly home.

Chapter 2

Flash Flood

It had been an unusually long, cold, harsh winter. Constant blowing snow and blizzards made living in Chicago claustrophobic for Israel Baker at times. Spring was near, according to the calendar hanging on his office wall. But as he looked out on the gray, flat day, he could sense spring was still hibernating. He longed to be out hiking among the washes, rocks, and granite hills of the desert southwest, where he could see vast distances in any direction and feel the heat of the intense yellow light warm his soul.

He loved living in Chicago and all that a big, vibrant city had to offer, but he also needed the endless space of the dry, isolated desert. He did not understand the hold the desert had on him, but every vacation that he could carve out of his demanding schedule, he headed to the Mojave Desert and spent days among the sand and silence, allowing it to feed his soul.. His friends thought he was nuts, even saying, "Who ever heard of a black man hiking and camping in the desert? You're crazy!" They teased him often.

A defense attorney who relished winning debates in the courtroom, he nevertheless could not articulate the thoughts and feelings the desert created in him. It was as if it had a secret to reveal only to him, and he needed to find out what it was. That secret, he hoped, would fill the constant emptiness that plagued him just outside his consciousness.

Never lacking for beautiful dates, he kept that empty, lonely feeling at bay by having an active social life. As a successful, single, attractive lawyer, he was never alone, and that kept his mind occupied. The only time he allowed the shadows to creep out from the recesses of his mind was when he was heading out to the desert to see if this time she would give her secret to him and close the hole in his heart.

Looking out his corner office window, barely able to see the high-rise building across from him due to yet another early spring snowstorm, Israel counted the days to when he would be landing in Las Vegas, renting a car, and heading out into his beloved desert. He hated Vegas and, being ever competitive, played a game with himself to see how quickly he could be off the plane, claim his luggage, catch the shuttle to the rental car lot, and be driving south on I-15 with Sin City in his rearview mirror. His best time so far had been forty-seven minutes. Damn good record.

Israel turned from the window and gave his focus to the stack of court files sitting on the corner of his expansive mahogany desk. He sat down in his leather chair and reached for the top file. *Only five more days before I can feel and see the sun again.* He gave a heavy sigh and turned to his computer to write his summary of the case he had just won.

~~~~

"Okay, kids, since it's Friday, it's time to clean out your desks for the weekend," Sally Dunkin announced from the front of her second grade classroom. "The buses and your parents will be here soon, and no one wants to stay at school over the weekend. Right?"

"No, Ms. Dunkin!" she heard the kids all yell as she watched them scurry to straighten their desks. *Me, either*, she thought. *As soon as you little hellions get out of here, I'm right behind you, heading for some peace and quiet.*

Sally Dunkin's car was already packed for her extended

weekend in the desert. She planned to drive out of the less-than-stimulating rat hole of a town where she lived and taught. Before nightfall, she would be in the vast openness of the Mojave Desert, watching for shooting stars and breathing in the expansive aroma of Mother Earth.

She had taken the teaching job in a town most people could not wait to get out of so that she could heed the call of being in the wilderness of the Southwest. The town and the job weren't too bad as long as she was able to get out into the desert. The hold it had on her was intoxicating, almost like being deeply in love and on her honeymoon. She wasn't married and never had been. No desire. The desert was her lover, and during the week, she longed for its embrace, the warmth of its breath, and the sparkle of its starlit eyes.

It made no sense for a curly-haired, cute, blond Florida cracker to long for sand, wind, and dryness, but she did, and she was good at following her heart. This listening to her soul had caused her to turn down two proposals of marriage over the last ten years: one from her surf-loving college boyfriend and the other from an incredibly handsome, ambitious principal from her first teaching job. *I am happy where I am*, she thought, as she wished somehow the desert could transform its qualities into the perfect man for her.

~~~

Israel watched the concrete runway get closer and closer.

He felt a quickening in his solar plexus as he thought of the Little Inn where he would be staying. By first light, he would be out exploring a new area of his playground. The wheels finally made contact with the ground, and he resisted the urge to unsnap his seat belt before the plane came to a complete stop.

~~~~

Sally restrained herself from speeding as she drove out of town. *Don't want to be delayed by a ticket,* she thought. The second she left the town's limits and headed down old Route 66, she opened the top of her Jeep and floored the gas pedal, feeling the warm, early evening wind in her hair and on her skin. Soon she would be where she always stayed when hiking the desert: at her friend Clyde's place in back of the watering hole he owned in the middle of nowhere.

After a decent sleep, Sally awoke to the gray of the early morning light filling the curtainless window. She immediately got up and began preparing to drive the twenty miles to her destination, a wash unnoticed by all those who flew down the road but seen by her numerous times as she drove to and from her outings. Each time she passed this little dip in the road, her focus was pulled to the wash, leading her eyes as far up as possible before the wash took a turn and led down a rocky slope. This time, heeding the call, she was going to hike for as long as it took to get to the end of it. She was prepared to spend the night if she had to, taking with her a camping backpack instead of just her day hiking pack.

~~~~

Up with the ringing of his phone alarm, Israel stocked his backpack with numerous water bottles and food for several days, along with the tools needed to spend the night out in the desert: a lightweight tarp, skullcap, jacket, gloves, long pants, flashlight, matches, pocketknife, water filter, and a compass. He was ready. He had seen a cut in the desert floor to the southeast that intrigued him each time he drove by it. Far in the distance, he could tell it led to a gentle slope, and that slope had called to him. He wanted to climb it and see what was on the other side. This was the day to do that.

~~~~

After hiking all day and being pulled deeper and deeper into the artery of the wash, Sally pushed on. Her hiking boots dug into the ever-softening sand. Her calves started to scream, and each step felt like trudging through slowly drying concrete. She was so tired. But something made her press on. A desire, a memory, a discovery?

Deciding to rest for the night before it got too dark to see, she made her way to the top of the wash and laid out her tarp, along with a lightweight thermal blanket, on the hard desert floor. She was smart enough to know not to sleep on the soft sand bed of the wash, where it would have been more comfortable but ever so dangerous if there were a flash flood.

Flash floods. They made her so nervous. Having lived in the desert for the past four years, she had seen several, and they scared her to her core. Along with the occasional earthquake, flash floods were the only negative about living in the desert. Being trapped, with water and sand roaring around and in her till she could no longer breathe, crushing and suffocating her in a slow death—just the thought caused her to panic. Each time she heard of a flash flood, her heart would stop, and she would have to talk herself out of a panic attack that would start to build from the depths of her soul.

She hated the way she feared those very rare desert occurrences, since she had no reason to dread them, having never experienced one, ever. *Just my crazy imagination,* she thought, as she pulled out her can of tuna from her backpack for dinner.

~~~~

Israel lay back on his tarp, having hiked all day. It felt good to be out of the Windy City. He gazed at the billions of stars in a moonless night, and every now and then, he glanced down into the shadowed wash he had been hiking. In the morning, he was going to descend back down and continue where he had climbed out for the night. He stretched out his long, muscular body, working out the kinks of the hike and feeling at home. As he watched the night sky, he let his hands scrape along the top of the sand, feeling the edges of the minute pebbles. Mother Earth was cooling down from the day.

I am safe, as long as there is no rain or flash flood, he thought as he drifted to sleep beneath a clear, starlit night. For some reason, flash floods made him extremely nervous.

~~~~

The warmth of the sharp, new morning sun woke the travelers from a renewing deep sleep that only the quiet of the desert landscape could offer. Yawning, bending, and stretching their stiff bodies from being on the ground all night, the two separate travelers packed up, cleared their campsites, and headed out toward destiny.

Hiking most of the day from opposite directions, the two very different people were unknowingly closing the gap between them. The travelers were lost in their own thoughts, listening to the subtle sounds of the desert against a backdrop of hues in pink, purple, gray, and brown.

They spotted each other on the distant horizon. Both were startled to see another person out in such a remote area of a remote desert. With eyes squinted against the brightness of the light, they did their best to size up each other as they continued to walk closer. Each found something familiar about the other. Odd. Both experienced a quickening of their hearts as they moved nearer.

As they continued to close the gap, they noticed a very old, half-submerged vehicle from the 1930s in the wash. The rusty top of the car beckoned them toward it. Reaching the car at the same time, they stared at each other for a moment, still surprised to find another human this far from civilization.

Sally was the first to speak. "Who are you?"

"Israel from Chicago," he replied. "You?"

"Sally." She spoke softly as she neared him and the car. "Do I know you?" she asked in confusion.

"I don't think so, but you look—well, feel—familiar," Israel said with some surprise.

By this point, each was standing across from the other with the wreck of the car between them. To break the awkwardness, they focused on the old car. The years of sand and water had worn the outside smooth, and in places, the sand and wind had blasted small holes along the outside of the car. The lid of the trunk had been torn off long ago. The back of the car contained less sand, so the two hikers could almost see the floor there. It held a half-exposed heavy metal box. They cleared the sand around the box, and Israel pulled it out of the back and laid it on the ground.

Sally opened the box. In it, they found a rock hound's tools. Israel picked up the chisel, as Sally laid her hand on the bumper of the car. The metal of the chisel and the metal of the car grabbed them both and pulled them into a terrifying memory.

Bright, sunny day. Hot wind blew in the open windows. Happy couple. Full of life. Honeymoon. *Honeymoon.* Yes, honeymoon flashed in their minds.

They had been married back East and were on their way to Los Angeles, where he was to be a geology professor. They had decided to explore the Mojave Desert as a part of their honeymoon so he could collect rocks and she could paint watercolor landscapes. They were happy, young, and deeply in love and had their whole lives in front of them. They did not notice the wall of water rushing out of the desert wash, coming right at them from the left. It hit them with such force the car flipped on its right side and shot down the wash, along with the other debris the water had picked up along its journey.

The young honeymooners fought for air, flailing their arms, trying to scream, only to have sand and water fill their mouths and lungs. The force of the water swept them out of the open windows, and their bodies tossed and turned like rag dolls being slung around by an evil kid. The rocks broke their bodies, and their remains washed along with the water. The car became stuck on a hard shelf, where over the decades more flash floods added debris and sand, waiting silently for a time to be discovered in the middle of nowhere.

Sally quickly pulled her hand off the car as Israel dropped the chisel.

"Eldon?" Sally questioned in a whisper as she looked at

Israel.

"Sara?" he responded slowly, looking wide-eyed at Sally.

They rushed into each other's arms, crying uncontrollably, hugging tightly, each trying to merge into the other. They grabbed at each other in a desperate attempt to be as close as possible to the other. They had revisited their past life in a nanosecond. Each finally understood the strong pull of the desert, the long weekend hikes, and the deep longing that had gripped their hearts all their lives.

They held on to each other for a very long time, neither wanting to be the first to break their hold. The sun slowly made its way to bed for the night, casting long shadows along the desert floor. With no need to talk, they broke their hold and silently prepared their bedding for the night next to the car. With their bodies intertwined as tightly as they could, they fell into a deep sleep under the dancing stars of the Mojave. Their hearts finally healed. The wound from a past life had been closed. The desert had called to them and led them back to each other.

Miles away, beyond the horizon, clouds had just emptied their bellies. Water was building up, gathering strength, and moving down a wash.

Chapter 3
Selkie Desert

The yellow-and-black Mini Cooper buzzed along the road like a giant bumblebee, whipping past Joshua trees, Mesquite bushes, and long vistas of desert flowers. Rich blue, stark orange, and bright red colors greeted her eyes everywhere she looked. The top was down on the Coop, and Maggie Martinez's nostrils were taking in the strong aroma the flowers were sending out in the air. At one point, the fragrances that permeated her nose shot forward a sharp memory from the recesses of her mind: *Colin.*

These flowers smell like Colin, she thought as she zipped down the road toward her destination. She was to be a bridesmaid in her cousin's wedding tomorrow. The rehearsal dinner was this evening.

Colin. Passionate memories of him soaked her mind, and with the aroma of the flowers to sharpen the images of their short time together, tears welled up in her eyes. She could smell him, feel his essence in every pore of her skin. His seeming nearness shook her to her core.

The intoxicating scent, the memories, the feelings were too overwhelming for her to continue driving on her journey. She pulled her car into the small dirt parking lot of a seldom-used hiking trail and got out. The desert called to her. She longed to be in the middle of the desert flowers and allow the thick perfume to take her back in time, to relive those precious days and nights three years ago.

Rather than resuming her drive, she got her hiking pack from the backseat, slung it over her shoulder, put on her hat, and headed down the path to a dense patch of desert flowers. It was early afternoon. She had plenty of time before she had to be at the rehearsal dinner.

Colin. She thought of him day and night, felt him with her mind and soul, bringing up the memory of the magic they had created during a great North Atlantic storm. His overwhelming male essence and the coziness of the cottage had warmed her to her very core. Oh, how she missed him, even as she remembered how he told her he would always be with her.

She found a large, flat boulder slightly off the trail among the flowers, perfect for stretching out and letting the sun soak her body as she traveled back in time to her trip to Ireland and her destiny with Colin.

~~~~

A forever single, thirty-something woman, Maggie had been with the tour group for the past six days, and she had grown sick of it. Mind you, the group was wonderful, and she had enjoyed getting to know some of the more colorful personalities. However, being the only semi-young single person in a nest of old couples, she grew tired of constantly being the third wheel. It was no different from when she was home. So when the group reached the Aran Islands, she could not resist the urge to rent a bicycle and take off on her own for a tour of solitude around the island.

With her lunch, made by the only inn on the island, secured in her knapsack, and the tour guide's warning to be back to the dock no later than 4:00 p.m. for the last boat back to the mainland, she grabbed the handlebars, slung her right leg over the back tire, and pushed off to new adventures.

~~~~

Collin McFadden looked out to the sea, watching the powerful, crashing waves beat against the chiseled rocks and cliffs that buffered the land from the harsh thrashing of the North Atlantic Sea. He never tired of the smell of the crisp spray of the salt water and the pungent smell of the seaweed that grew along the shoreline. It was his first memory, and it always brought him security and tranquility.

He turned his tall, toned body away from the sea, and with his charcoal-black eyes, surveyed the moor of craggy rocks and thick patches of grass and heather that stretched to the horizon. It always amazed him how humans had somehow managed to eke out a living on this harsh land. But they had for thousands of years, and he admired that. He stood, head tilted toward the sea mist, meditating, taking in the land and horizon, loving all he felt and inhaled, as his shaggy shiny black hair danced in the wind.

~~~~

Maggie headed north along the only road the island offered, being careful to remember that cars drove on the wrong side of the road here. She had little to worry about, as there were few cars on the island. There were mostly horses, buggies, and bicycles. Every so often, she came upon a cottage or passed a buggy with a driver who gave her a friendly nod. Sometimes she came upon other tourists, whom she avoided at all cost.

She had come to Ireland to get to know the land and the people of her mother's ancestors. After several years saving for this trip, the last thing she wanted to do was share it with other tourists or hang out where they were. She wanted to *feel* what it was like to be a local.

She did not understand the draw she had to the Emerald Isle. Just that it had been a pull on her soul for a very long time. Maybe being half-Irish had something to do with it. Maybe not, but finally one of her dreams had been fulfilled.

~~~~

Wind loved this area of Earth as well, blowing up huge swells of seawater along the shorelines and creating some of the most pregnant clouds and violent storms ever known to man along the coast. Inland, in contrast, Wind tended to give only mist and gentle rain.

Spring was Wind's favorite time of year, and Wind loved displaying its many creative ways of saturating and sculpturing the land. Wind took time to create the vast clouds and then fill them with moisture, turning all shades of gray, and then unleashing their water-filled bellies on the terra below.

~~~~

Maggie had ridden her bicycle along the coastal road, losing track of time, stopping often to take a picture or just gaze at the horizon with her chestnut eyes, unaware of the growing storm that Wind was busy creating.

Wind, forever blowing, began to get stronger. Fat drops of rain startled her, and she looked up from taking a picture of lichen on a rock to see the storm coming in. She had to find shelter fast. The sky was turning dark quickly. She stood up, looking around for the best place to get out of the impending storm, when she saw him.

He was coming up a trail from the edge of the cliff with a bundle under his arm. She caught her breath. He was a vision of male beauty: tall, dark, and very fit. Wind blew his stark white shirt open, revealing toned muscles that made her breath come faster. She watched this Adonis brush away the long, dark hair that whipped around his handsome face as he grabbed at his shirt. He bowed his head against Wind. Maggie was transfixed. This Celtic druid was breathtaking.

~~~~

Colin, his eyes squinting, looked into the gust. Forever familiar with the patterns of weather, he knew a violent storm was coming in fast. He stooped down, picked up the huge pelt of dark brown fur that lay next to his feet, rolled it up, and placed it safely under his arm.

He stepped carefully along the rock outcropping, enjoying how his feet connected to the solid earth, then looked up and saw her. Beautiful and tall, with long, raven-black hair blowing across her face, she was scanning the land looking for shelter. Something about her posture, a sense of strength mixed with innocence, made his heart race.

Through Wind's whistling, he yelled to get her attention and motioned for her to come to him. He had shelter. He pointed to the indentation of a small grotto, which was imprinted into the pile of rocks about a hundred yards to his left.

~~~~

Hearing the man's deep, strong voice cut through the gale, Maggie understood his gestures and started running toward where he pointed. She reached the outcropping after he did, shivering and soaked to the bone from the storm.

He waited for her with the pelt open to receive her. She noticed his eyes fall on her full breasts through her soaked shirt. She tucked her head down, stepped into the dark grotto, and allowed him to wrap her in the fur.

She felt protected, wrapped not only with him in the fur but in the strange man's strong arms. Safe, that was what she felt. This was not like her. She never trusted strangers and, God forbid, never ever followed one anywhere. Yet here she was, in a foreign country, no less, in the middle of an isolated island, under rocks, wrapped in fur, next to a gorgeous man she did not know. And yet she felt like she was home. Her mother would roll over in her grave if she knew.

"Hi, I'm Colin." His thick Irish accent filled her ears with song and made her skin tingle.

She turned to face him and caught her breath. His eyes drew her in and made her head swirl. "I'm Maggie." The words came hard between the gasps for air, not so much from being out of breath from running, but more from being overcome by his strong male essence.

"Are ye okay? Our storms can really knock a person around. Are ye warm?" His caring tone penetrated her very being. It warmed her more than the fur blanket did, but she was not going to let him know.

"Yes, I'm getting warm. Thank you." She couldn't say much more, still swirling from him being so close to her. And those eyes of his! They were like deep wells of mystery and seduction. She could feel he was still looking at her.

Inhaling his unique fragrance, she dared to lay her head on his chest as she looked out at the raging storm. It had been so long since she had taken in the smell of a man that being so close to one almost made her pass out. He rested his head on top of hers and watched the storm with her. Their bodies perfectly fit like two pieces of a puzzle. They were filled with an emotion neither understood.

~~~~~

Wind matched their emotions, stirring up more gale and fury. It made the earthlings pull together even closer. Wind was pleased with the creation of the storm and what it had done for these humans.

~~~~

Eventually the storm quieted, but Colin knew better. It was not over. It was just getting started. This time of year, storms like this could rage for days, playing havoc with all it came in contact with. He could tell by the twisting and turning of the clouds and the hard piercing of the rain that this was going to be one of those meaner storms.

"The cottage I'm staying in is just a stone's throw from here. Let's go before the next phase of this storm gets us, and we end up here all night!" he yelled over Wind's howl.

The idea of being so close to him all night created a smile across her face and sent a shiver through her body. She reached for his outstretched hand and ran with him to a small cottage sitting along the edge of a cliff.

The interior of the one-room cottage was warm, lit by the fire from the small fireplace in the corner of the kitchen side of the room. The mood of the cottage was right out of the tour posters she had seen of homes in Ireland. She felt secure and grateful to be out of the storm, yet so alive being close to a man who captured her very breath and brought moisture between her legs.

She stood in the middle of the room with the fur wrapped tightly around her. Desperately doing her best to warm up, she watched this Celtic god bring the fire in the fireplace to roaring life. He stood up, slowly turned toward her, took her in from head to toe with his black eyes as he walked toward her.

Colin reached for the fur, pulling it ever so slowly off her shoulders while penetrating her with his mesmerizing eyes. Maggie shivered in the heat of the cabin. He did not stop there, but continued removing her soaked blouse, shorts, and shoes. She did not stop him, nor did she want him to stop, as he removed her wet bra with one hand and reached up with his other hand to cup her breast. His lips moved to suckle the other breast. She cried out, arched her back, and opened herself to this stranger. Colin stroked her back, feeling the curve of her spine, cupping the fullness of her hips, and lifting her to connect with him.

Her flesh responded to his touch with goose bumps. He smiled. She returned his touch, caressing his shoulders, feeling his taut, smooth back while taking in his kiss, feeling his lips and the deep thrust of his tongue. Still connected, he carried her ever so gently to the bed across the room. He softly laid her on it and placed himself on top of her.

Maggie had never in her life experienced such a sensual touch as what Colin gave her when he stroked the mound of her breast with his finger, lightly settling on the nipple. He softly pinched, as he thrust his tongue deep in her mouth and at the same time penetrated her vessel even deeper. She arched to meet him as she screamed out in pleasure.

A seductive whisper filled her left ear. "You will come for

me many times before this storm is through, lass."

She hugged his back tightly, arching higher as his strong hands grabbed her tight buttocks, pulling her up to him as he came down in her. An explosive moan came up from the depth of his soul as he flooded her with his essence.

They held each other in soft love, listening to each of their heartbeats returning to a resting rate, as the storm howled its piercing noise just outside the cottage. Wrapped in each other's bodies like a Celtic knot, they shared the feeling of having known each other across lifetimes. No words needed to be said. Their higher selves knew, and there was no need for superficial verbiage.

For days, while Wind orchestrated the storm outside, the human creatures explored each other with abandonment, stopping only to eat and rest. Laughter and deep moans could be heard from time to time above the roaring of the storm just outside of the tiny thatched-roof cottage.

Curled up by the fire, eating mutton jerky, he told her of his large extended family, how they were all fishermen and fisherwomen. They were on the sea now looking for food. He would have been with them but loved to be on land this time of the year, so had taken a short holiday.

Snuggling closer to him as they lay by the warm fire, Maggie told him how she was an only child and grew up listening to her mother's stories of her relatives who came from

Ireland to America during the last great potato famine. As she grew, so did a strong desire to visit the Emerald Isle someday.

~~~~

Wind watched the two beings interact, knowing the softness of their joy and tenderness of their touch would travel like an infectious fragrance on Wind's rain. Wind continued to blow and rain with delight, but eventually Wind grew tired. The job was done.

~~~~

After four magical days, Maggie woke to birds singing and the sun shining. Now familiar with Colin's protective form lying next to her while she slept, she became acutely aware that he was not beside her. She reached over and touched his side of the bed softly, only feeling the coolness of its emptiness. Panic set in. She looked to where his now-familiar form had been and saw the package and note lying in his place.

My dear Maggie,

It tears my heart out that I must leave you and return to the sea. My life and my heart will ever be with you. These past few magical days will be etched forever on my soul. I will always know where you are, and you will always be with me, as I know I will always be with you. Whenever you look to the sea, please think of me and the love we have for each other, as it is timeless. I have left you a physical piece of myself to add to your memories of our short but deep time spent together, a part of me that wrapped you in warmth the first day we met.

Forever and always,
Colin

Maggie opened the wrapped package that accompanied the letter and saw he had cut a small patch of fur from the blanket he had wrapped them in during the storm on the first day they had met. It was an odd gift. She held it to her cheek and felt the soft fur next to her skin. She breathed in the rugged sweet smell it emitted. It reminded her of his scent. She cried harder. She would cherish it forever, carrying it with her wherever she went.

After some time, she came out of her grief, cleared her swollen eyes, and stood up. She looked around the room of the cottage, smiling and blushing, remembering the tender moments of lovemaking, the meals they shared as the storm raged on, the conversations they had, and again the coupling, which their bodies could not get enough of.

Maggie gently folded the letter inside of the patch of fur, rolled it up, and placed it deep in her pocket. After looking around one last time, she softly closed the door, slowly got on the bicycle, and headed away from the cottage.

Once on the boat heading back to the mainland, she knew she would soon be back with the tour group. With a breaking heart, she looked out to the sea as the land faded into the mist.

Off in the distance she saw a group of seals. Watching them took her mind off the pain of missing Colin. She noticed one seal in particular move away from the group and come closer to the boat. Other people on the ferry took notice, and a group of tourists joined her to watch these beauties of the sea.

The lone seal came closer to the boat and moved directly in front of where Maggie was looking. She watched the seal with interest, as it seemed he was watching her. His eyes were a deep black like Colin's.

She knew this was crazy. She was just missing Colin. She was not thinking straight. The patch of fur was in her coat pocket. She got it out to stroke her face with it and take in its aroma again. As she did, the lone seal came alongside the boat right under where she was standing. He made a leap out of the sea and flopped on his back, revealing a patch of fur missing from his underbelly near his heart, the same size of the fur she had in her hand. She gasped and started to cry and laugh all at the same time. People looked at her oddly.

She now knew who Colin truly was and why he had to return to the sea. He was a selkie. Growing up she never tired of her mother telling her stories of Ireland, especially the stories about Selkies. Seals that have the ability to transform into humans. If a person is lucky enough to find where the Selkie had stored its fur, the selkie could never return to the sea without it. Selkies made devoted lovers even as they longed for the sea.

She waved and threw a kiss to the seal with her left hand, as she held the patch of fur to her heart with the other. The seal made one more leap and then rejoined the rest of the seals waiting for him off in the distance. She watched till she could not see him any longer, then reluctantly turned her back to the sea, still holding the fur to her heart.

~~~~

A shadow crossed Maggie's face, momentarily blocking out the sun. It jarred her to the present. She opened her eyes to see the sun hanging low in the west. A few clouds had formed in the sky during the time her body lay on the boulder while her soul revisited Ireland. She sat up, aware that hours had passed by in minutes. She scanned the vast sky to the horizon. With a start, she realized the few clouds in the sky had formed the shape of a seal.

"Remember, I will always be with you, lassie," she heard Colin whispering to her from the past. She pulled the patch of fur from her pack and held it to her heart as she watched the form of the seal cloud fade into other shapes.

Maggie reluctantly got up from the boulder, thanked Mother Earth for this time of memory, tucked the fur into her shirt near her heart, and walked back to her car. A light breeze blew a soft, fresh memory in her mind and a new feeling in her soul. Maggie started the engine of her Mini Coop, pulled out onto the road, and continued her journey.

In a couple of hours, she would be in the company of the wedding party enjoying the rehearsal dinner and free-flowing drinks her cousin was providing for the group.

Among the waiters preparing to serve the group was a handsome, dark-haired Irishman waiting for a raven-haired bridesmaid to arrive.

Chapter 4

Seeds

Melting in the blazing hot Nevada sun at the Park and Wait lot at McCarran International Airport, Wendy waited for her daughter to call to let her know which terminal to pick her up from. She was nervous. Turning the AC on from time to time so she would not melt, she thought of the last time she had seen or spoken to her daughter, Natlee. *What was it, four years ago? Oh my God, no. It has been almost seven years ago.* The realization brought sharp, biting sadness.

Seven years ago, Wendy's ex-husband surprised her by showing up at her front door telling her he was there to get Natlee. With the child standing behind her, he directed Natlee to get her things while Wendy stood there in complete shock.

Mark explained that Natlee had called him a week before complaining that her mom had been mean to her. She had hit Natlee for no reason, and Natlee wanted her dad to come get her. So the two of them, Mark and fourteen-year-old Natlee, had made arrangements for Natlee to live with him without including her, the child's mother. She was furious and felt deeply betrayed and abandoned, and she let him know it.

Calmly, in his typical manner, Mark responded, "Her decisions override your decisions. You know that, don't you?"

"Yes, Mark, with you that's true. But how is that serving her to her highest good?" Wendy asked intensely, looking him in the eye and waiting for a response that never came.

She could not believe it. She could not wrap her brain around what she had just been told. When she was able to catch her breath but still in shock from seeing him standing on her porch, at her front door, all the way from Texas, she asked him why hadn't he called her to get her side of the story? His response was distant, with no emotion, like he was on one of his military missions, "There will be no hitting."

"I agree with you, Mark, but did she tell you she grabbed the steering wheel while I was driving on the freeway because she was angry with me for not allowing her to stay out past curfew? My hand flew up and hit her hand to get it away from the wheel. I was keeping her from causing us to have a wreck, from getting us killed. Did she tell you that? No! Your precious little princess never does anything wrong." Hard tears had washed down her face as she lost control and screamed the choked words out to the only man she had ever truly loved.

Wendy felt deeply. The anger, hurt, betrayal, and confusion only compounded when she saw her daughter come downstairs with two packed suitcases and walk past her and out the door with the smug attitude that only a red-blooded American teenaged girl could have toward her mother. And without saying a word or even looking back at her, they'd left.

For days, weeks, and months, Wendy had cried, mentally beaten herself, and blamed herself for being too hard on her only child. When she had called to see how her daughter was doing, her ex was polite but cold. When she talked to Natlee, it was like pulling hen's teeth to get her to say anything. Slowly, over time, the distance between calls became wider and wider, till Wendy had no contact with her daughter at all. It left a huge hole in her heart.

Eventually, as years passed, she was able to soften her outlook on how she had raised her daughter. Talking to friends helped. So did the two-hundred-dollar-an-hour shrink. Over time, she realized that all of "this stuff" was part of a higher plan. At some level, she and her daughter, and even her ex, had made a contract in this lifetime for this upside-down triangle to play out. She just wished her human self knew the answer.

God, it is so hot, not even the devil would live here, she thought as she brought her attention back to the present and reached for the button to blast the AC again. Her cell phone rang. "Natlee, I can't wait to see you. Which terminal are you at?" She tried not to sound too excited or anxious. It was hard, but after all, it had been seven years.

As Wendy pulled out of the Park and Wait, she thought over the last seven years. She had learned whenever she caught herself thinking of her daughter, which was at the very least once a day, to send her light and love. She visualized her surrounded by a protective bubble. She chose to see Natlee as a strong, responsible, successful, and happy young adult. All of this made Wendy feel better.

When she caught herself thinking of all the negative things that had taken place, she told herself not to go down that path again. It only led to self-hatred, and she no longer wanted to live like a victim. Over time, the practice paid off. She was beginning to live her life without the need for her daughter to be in it.

Driving to Terminal 2, Wendy marveled at the turn of events that had taken place within the last month. She had gotten a call from her daughter out of the blue, asking if they could go together to her cousin's wedding in California. Natlee acted on the phone like they had just talked the other day. Wendy struggled to keep from crying. The call had knocked her off-center. After all, she had spent the last seven years working on being centered, forgiving herself, and not being a doormat to others.

"Of course I would love to have you come along. You haven't seen this side of your family in a very long time." Deep breaths helped her stay calm in her conversation with her almost twenty-two-year-old daughter.

It was decided. Natlee would fly from her home in Miami, and Wendy from Denver to Vegas. They would meet up, and then they would drive to a little desert town for the family wedding. It would be a three-hour drive, traveling along a very isolated two-lane road.

Was it a chance to mend their relationship or make it worse? Wendy did not know, but she was willing to take the leap. After all, it was Natlee who had called, not her. She had given up long ago when her calls were not answered or returned.

She remembered telling herself, *now, don't anticipate how the trip will go or get too excited about seeing your daughter again. Don't get disappointed if Natlee backs out at the last minute. Just stay in the moment and think good positive thoughts.* Wendy breathed deeply, which assisted calming her core. After the call, she went for a meditative walk to ground her good thoughts. That had been a month ago.

Pulling up to the curb, it was easy for Wendy to pick out her daughter from the hordes of travelers with their luggage.

Natlee was a carbon copy of Wendy when she was twenty-one. Natlee had a long ponytail to her waist, and her posture Wendy recognized from pictures of her own self at that age.

Does Natlee have any children? she wondered out of the blue as she watched her daughter for the first time in a long time and revisited memories of Natlee over the years growing up. She would have to ask but at the right time. She reminded herself that her daughter was an adult and this was a possible new beginning, a tabula rasa, a clean slate.

~~~~

At the curb, Wendy got out of her car and yelled to Natlee while waving her hand. Natlee looked to where the voice called her name. She had no problem picking out her mother. *She looks just like Grandma*, Natlee thought with great surprise. *My mother's hair is turning gray*. This revelation shocked her a bit. Her mother was getting old even though she was only forty-eight, or was it forty-nine? Or was she now fifty? Natlee could not remember.

~~~~

It was a bit awkward when the two women met. Both were not quite sure whether to hug or shake hands. Both gave out the same nervous, light laugh. Wendy quickly hugged her daughter and asked how her trip was. Wendy asked was there anything Natlee needed before they headed out into the heart of the Mojave. As she stooped down to pick up Natlee's luggage,

Natlee shook her head no.

With Natlee's luggage in the trunk along with hers, Wendy pulled out of the terminal and headed toward I-15. By the time Wendy got her nerve up to speak again, Natlee had pulled out her phone, brought up her playlist, put plugs in her ears, leaned back, and closed her eyes to listen to the music. In a way, Wendy was relieved, but in another way, she was irritated. Her daughter's attitude was the same as when she had been a teenager and they had taken trips together. Then Wendy remembered: tabula rasa. *Shift focus,* she thought. *She is just as nervous as I am, and this makes her feel more secure. Just be grateful she is here. She is here, right next to you. Your daughter is within your sight*, her mind told her as she almost started crying. One of her prayers had been answered.

Wendy took the south ramp onto I-15, pressed the gas pedal a bit harder, and headed into the blazing eye of the sun. She concentrated on the traffic the freeway carried and the many two- and three-trailer rigs heading to LA or San Diego.

After she blasted past several, she settled into a grove and was able to steal a look at her daughter. Natlee seemed to be asleep. Wendy could still see the child she'd raised hidden in the lines and curves of a grown young woman. The turned-up nose, high cheekbones, and long eyelashes were the same, but the face was a bit more mature. Her heart sang because her daughter was here, next to her.

A little over an hour had passed, yet the sun was still high in the sky. Natlee continued sleeping as Wendy turned off the freeway onto a shoulder-less, two-lane highway leading deeper into the heart of the desert. She loved driving this stretch of road when she returned home for visits. The vast, pinto-colored desert mountains soothed her soul. She never could quite express in words what this landscape did to and for her, how it made her feel, how it filled up her cells with new energy, new light, and new hope. She was grateful for every grain of sand that Spirit had molded into these mountains, valleys, dry lakes, and washes. She was grateful for this vista at this very moment.

When she had turned off onto the two-lane road, she silently called upon the life force of the land she loved so much to support her at this time, in this place, with her daughter. She asked the spirits of the occupants of the vast vista to hold them in love and light and to send healing energy to their relationship.

Finally, she heard stirring to her right. Natlee was waking up. Wendy glanced over and witnessed déjà vu. It was as if she were looking back in time into another trip on this very same road with a much younger Natlee.

Squinting her eyes as she sat upright in her seat, Natlee asked her mother, "How long have I been sleeping?"

"Not long. You so remind me of when we took this same trip ten years ago. Do you remember?" she asked cheerfully.

76

"Oh God, Mom, must you bring up the past?"

"I was just reminded of when you were eleven years old. You fell asleep on this very same road. You woke up, looked around, and asked if we were there yet, and it brought back some great memories . . ." Her voice trailed off, fearful the conversation was heading into a familiar pattern she was unwilling to repeat.

A snort of a sound came from the passenger side of the car. Wendy decided it was best to ignore it. *Be grateful she is here. Let her lead the direction this reunion is to go*, she thought, reminding herself of the blank slate analogy.

They were now driving in a concentrated area of Joshua trees. Wendy chose to put her focus on them. The larger ones were several hundred years old. She had tried to grow them in her home in Highlands Ranch, but they only grew to about five inches, barely as high as a blade of grass, before they died. She marveled at the smaller ones, wondering how they could grow into such large trees.

She was also acutely aware of her daughter next to her. *When had she moved to Miami?* she pondered. She so desperately wanted to find out how Natlee's life was going, what she was doing, how she was doing, and what made her reach out in the first place. *Patience*, Wendy told herself. *Patience.*

Time moved by slowly even as she drove ninety miles an

hour on this lonely road. The silence in the car grew so thick that Wendy had a hard time breathing. Even with the AC on high, the air was thick as a brick. She fought back, wanting to say something, but what? There was so much to say and yet nothing to say. There was so much to ask and yet nothing to ask. Frustration started to swell up in her. She could feel that the same thing was taking place in Natlee also. They were just alike, her daughter had told her once just before she left to live with her dad. Wendy had to agree. Maybe that was why their relationship had been so volatile.

"Mom, slow down. You're driving way too fast," Natlee scolded harshly.

"I know what I am doing. I do not need you or anyone else to tell me how to drive. I drove long before you were born!" The words flew out of her mouth, with no thought to them. Too late to catch them and stuff them back into her mouth. Old patterns died hard.

"I knew it was a mistake to do this. God, nothing has changed. You are still the same old bitch I remember growing up!" Natlee screamed at her mother.

Wendy jerked the car to a sharp stop, almost flipping the car in the soft sand as she slammed on the brakes. She yelled back at her daughter as dust engulfed the car, "You were the most difficult child to raise: never sleeping, always thinking you were equal to adults, never listening to me, and doing what you wanted. And your dad supported you!" She shouted at her only daughter, regretting the outburst even as she spoke the words, but she was powerless to stop it from happening. Old habits die hard.

"Don't bring Dad into this!" Natlee pressed nose to nose with her mom, like a mirror looking at itself from different timelines. She turned, opened the door, and started walking out into the desert.

Wendy opened her door and followed her. Catching up to her, she reached for Natlee's arm and cried out, "What is wrong with us? What did I do to make you so angry with me?"

Natlee whipped around, jerking her arm away from her mother's as she shouted, "You were never there for me! You were always working and stressed out. You were never in a good mood." Natlee turned back and continued walking away from her mother.

"Well, you were a high-maintenance kid, always pushing, pushing, pushing to get whatever you wanted, never sleeping through the night your first two years of life, and I was so tired, so exhausted from raising you on my own and working!" Wendy screamed out seven years of pent-up frustration. She reached out to grab her daughter's arm again to get her to turn around and stop walking farther away from the car and deeper into the blistering desert.

Natlee whipped around and hit her mother squarely in the

jaw. Wendy punched back. World War III had broken out in the middle of nowhere. Anyone driving by would have thought it was comedy hour at the mud-wrestling pit. Two women, one young and the other middle-aged, dressed sharply, duking it out in the bleak, blinding desert was a sight one does not often see.

The two women went at it, swinging with passion, vomiting years of pent-up frustration at each other. All their accumulated anger, disappointment, and misunderstanding of each other came pouring out, hurled at each other with such viciousness that their voices bounced off the nearby mountains and came back at them, their words penetrating each other to the depths of their souls.

Both fell to the sand at the same time, crying. They were exhausted from the release of all the poison that had built up in their cells and minds over the years. Finally, there was silence. Both breathed hard, not speaking. Each looked down to where they had fallen, as the desert slowly started to heal the deep wound in their souls.

Still looking down at the ground and playing with the sparkling sand, picking it up and letting it fall gently between her fingers over and over, Wendy spoke softly. "I was in my twenties when I had you. I was scared. I was, in a way, still a child myself. Your dad left me when you were two years old. I was afraid and just went into survival mode. Please forgive me. I closed down, afraid that if I loved you too much you would go away also."

Silence persisted between them. Wendy continued to watch the sand fall between her fingers, watch the sun glisten against the cut angles of the grains of sand. A gentle breeze kept the penetrating sun from frying them.

~~~~

Natlee looked at her stockings, torn by the needles of the bushes they had been fighting in. She saw the sparkling sand near her knees. She took in what her mother had just said. She listened for the first time to a woman, not her mother, but a woman just like her, for she understood. She was scared also.

Finally Natlee spoke. "Mom, I'm sorry also. I realize now, as I get older, you did your best. I was so angry you and Dad were not together, and I blamed you." She paused. "I guess you were just safer." Natlee looked over at her mom and saw for the first time in her life, a woman, like her, not a mother, but a woman, just like her, making her way the best she could in this world.

~~~~

Wendy looked at her daughter. She listened to Natlee's words and saw the softening in her daughter's eyes, the relaxed posture of her shoulders, and the release of tension in her body. Wendy felt grateful.

Both came to awareness at about the same time as to what had just taken place, taking in the sight of a swollen lip on one and a black eye on the other. A healing of sorts had started to take place but in a most surprising and shocking way. They noticed each other's tangled hair, streaked mascara, and broken fingernails. They each surveyed their surroundings and then looked at their own appearance. And then they started to laugh at the stupidity that had just taken place. They belly-laughed till they cried, getting up and reaching out to hug each other. They apologized, saying how much they loved and missed each other and how grateful they were that they had come back together.

With arms around each other, they walked slowly back to the car, each a bit lighter, each healed a bit deeper, and each a bit happier. The desert had offered them a new beginning, and in their souls, they accepted this new beginning with gratitude.

Neither said a word as they dusted themselves off before getting into the car and driving on toward their destination. In the silence, deep peace enveloped the two women. The air was light. The sky turned brighter, even as the sun set lower in the horizon. They drove on, each with her own thoughts. A new beginning was forming between the two women.

In the distance, they saw a building situated in a valley, a watering hole for the locals, the Desert Gator. Wendy pulled into the gravel lot and parked. Neither had spoken since continuing their journey thirty minutes prior. "Let's go in, freshen up, and have a drink. Sound good?" she asked.

Natlee nodded in agreement.

They opened the door to the eclectic, rundown establishment. A few of the local barflies sat at the bar, and a couple sat at a table to the right of the door. Natlee watched one of the barflies check out her mom. He looked to be between their ages, and she could tell he was on the hunt for a sugar mama. She gave him a snarly look, as she followed her mom to the left, heading to the bathroom to clean up.

Sitting at a table opposite the bar, Wendy sipped a scotch, and Natlee, a light beer. Natlee asked her mom, "Why are mother and daughter relationships so complicated sometimes?"

Wendy took a stiff drink and surveyed the bar and its aging interior. Her eyes took in the silver-haired, fat-bellied owner behind the bar talking to one of the regulars and then looked back down at the gold liquid in her glass. Finally she spoke. "I guess because when you were a seed in me, I was a seed in my mom, as she was a seed in her mother. The roots of mothers and daughters go deep and are so intertwined, they sometimes can be complicated."

The two women sat for a while, taking in the profound truth of the idea, each with her own enlightened thoughts. Finally, looking up from their thoughts, each caught the other's eye, and they softly smiled at the mirror.

They finished their drinks, silently got up, and headed out the door. Their new journey, their new relationship, had just begun. Natlee touched her mom gently on the shoulder as they made their way to the car. Wendy turned around and faced her daughter. With a big smile and tears in her eyes, Natlee said ever so sweetly, "Mom, I'm pregnant."

Chapter 5
Barfly

Peter reached up and grabbed the naturally formed handhold of the rough granite. His energy almost spent, fingers aching and thighs quivering, with the last of his resources almost gone, he lifted himself up.

"Why did I choose to climb this rock outcropping, so damn far away from the road, so damn hard to get to?" he grumbled as his thoughts beat him up.

Lugging all the climbing equipment to reach the area made it almost not worth tackling, but it was a fantastic rock to climb. It was a seven-pointer, and due to the difficulty of getting to it, most climbers avoided this section, even in an area known for some of the best climbing in the world. By the time they got to the bottom of Pigeon Hole, they were exhausted from hiking through the thick, soft sand while weighed down with heavy climbing equipment.

However, the reward was intoxicating. No other climbers to get in one's way. The view was to die for. And of course, one would have bragging rights for having climbed a seven-pointer.

He couldn't wait to tell the gang at Desert Gator about the climb. The guys always seemed to relish hearing of his adventures and admire him for his climbing skills.

He had decided to get away and think about his future, something he rarely did. Thinking was not one of his strong suits. He had chosen this climb so he could clearly think without anyone bothering him. And he had a lot to think about. The most important and urgent, should he ask Sheila to marry him or not? It scared the shit out of him, but how else was he going to survive once his uncle died? Where would he live? How would he live? He had always depended on others to take care of him.

Normally he never gave a rat's ass about his future, relying on the wiles of the wind to carry him wherever. Except for all the failed relationships with selfish bitches he seemed to get involved with, this way of living had worked for him for forty-four years. But unfortunately, at this stage in the game of life, he was starting to run out of options, and it made him very uncomfortable and grumpy.

Reaching for the next ledge, he pulled his toned body up higher. *I do love her—I really do. She is just like me, a very generous person*, he thought with a weary smile as he pulled himself up over the top of Pigeon Hole. *Made it.*

His chest heaving from the challenging climb, Peter triumphantly sat, dangling his feet over the edge, taking in the surrounding desert landscape, and feeling elated about his accomplishment. He reached in his backpack for the second of four beers he had brought with him along with the flask of whiskey. He took a deep drink of beer and set it down. Creases formed on his forehead when he remembered the conversation he and Sheila had the last time they were together. *She's wrong, but she just won't admit it. I don't drink that much, not like some people I know. Besides, if she knew me when I was younger, I could really put away the beer.* Smiling, he remembered his wild, weird younger days. What fun! "Women can be such pains in the ass," he sighed, "but they are nice to cuddle with in bed." He took another long, satisfying drink of the semicold beer followed by a little shot of Jameson's.

Concentrating on the list of reasons for marrying her, he continued with his thoughts. *We do have a lot in common. She's athletic like me, loves to hike and camp like I do. I enjoy teaching her to climb, and she's a quick learner. We have great debates, and she loves to argue with me, which makes me hornier than hell.* He chuckled. *For being older than me, her body is in prime shape. Being a long-distance runner has paid off for her. Sex was one of the many benefits of being with her. She was indeed a great lover.* Peter tingled remembering some of the places where they had made love.

Over the two years they had been together, they had traveled to Peru, Greece, and Australia, as well as numerous places in the States on her dime. He was so blessed to have her in his life. She loved to travel like he did, and she had the means to do so, whereas he didn't. He had never made that kind of money in his entire life. He was so fortunate to have found her, and even better than that, *She's crazy about me. And why not? I'm a good catch*, he thought, as he coiled the new climbing rope she had given him the previous week. He took another deep swig of whiskey.

Taking in the beauty of the desert, the shapes and formations that made up this labyrinth of excellent climbing, he finished the last of his beer, crushed the can, and placed it in his now-lighter backpack. He pissed off the back edge of the pinnacle, slung his pack over his shoulder, descended down the back side of Pigeon Hole, and headed toward his truck. He was looking forward to pounding down a really cold one before meeting up with her at her cabin. He could almost feel the sharp taste wash down his throat.

Yes, I am lucky, but should I ask her to marry me? All I

have to offer her is myself.

Deep in thought and edgy from the dilemma of not having come to a conclusion, he continued toward his truck, hoping to decide before he met up with her. *What if I ask and she says no, then what happens to our relationship? I know she doesn't want to live together.*

That was the core of his concern. What would happen to him if she said no? Or if he did not ask her, what would happen to him when he had to leave his uncle's home once he died? And by the looks of it, his uncle was going to pass sooner rather than later. What would happen? A gulp or two of Jameson's helped him to not think so hard on it. He didn't want to get a migraine.

Finally reaching his truck, he drained the last of the whiskey, threw his backpack in the back, got in the front, and blasted the AC. Cool air washed over him. He reached in the glove box for a fresh pack of Camels and realized it was his last pack. Pissed, he pounded his fists on the dash. *Shit. Shit. Shit. My last pack. I just bought four packs the day before yesterday. Why does this always happen to me?* Groaning, he banged his head on the steering wheel.

Get a grip. You promised Sheila you would work on your anger, he reminded himself. Taking a deep breath and then another one, he started to relax.

If he only bought a couple of beers and no more, he would

have enough money to buy one pack. He just hoped Sheila had stocked the cabin for him. If not, he would have to make that one pack last all weekend. He started to get irritated again. A deep drag filled his body with nicotine. He took another and began to calm down. A cold drink would add to the calmness. Maybe Clyde would let him put a pack or two on his bill. After all, Peter was one of Clyde's best customers, and Sheila always paid off his bill when they went to the bar.

The bright turquoise siding of the Desert Gator popped into view on the horizon. Peter focused on the shine of the sun reflecting off the metallic paint, and he calculated how long before he'd pull into the parking lot. The building was a good ten miles away. It stood out like a bruise among the Joshua trees and Mesquite. At night, the building glowed with psychedelic images when car lights hit the siding. Clyde had a warped sense of humor.

Since moving to the desert to take care of his aging ailing uncle, Peter had found the watering hole to be a source of friendship. He loved to sit at one end of the bar and converse with the patrons. He had, over the past five years, gotten to know some of the regulars and enjoyed talking to the tourists who stopped in from around the world, having found the place through an offbeat tourist book, *The Weirdest Watering Holes of the World*.

The Desert Gator had made it into the book not because of

the psychedelic siding, though that would have qualified, but because of Ol' Gate, a twenty-foot ancient toothless alligator who lived out back behind the bar. People could actually pet him. So word spread, and the bar thrived in the middle of nowhere.

The décor of the bar started with items from the worldly travels of the Australian owner. Over the years, people had donated their own quirky castoffs, transforming the bar into an eclectic museum of junk.

Peter slammed the door of his uncle's old Ford truck, leaned against it, pulled out his folded wad of money from his right front pocket, and counted it with sharp pulls, as if he had hundred dollar bills instead of eleven ones and a ten. Damn, just enough for a couple of drinks and maybe a pack of cigarettes. He had hoped he had miscounted and actually had more, but no such luck. Crap. Oh well, such was life.

Standing inside the entrance, he took a minute to allow his eyes to adjust slightly to the darkness of the bar. Familiar with his second home, he ducked under the buffalo head mounted over the doorway leading to the vast room that made up the main portion of the bar. He headed to his favorite seat, and by the time he parked his lazy butt on the stool, his favorite beer was popped open and waiting for him. *I like the service I get here. They treat me well.* He smiled and gave a hearty hello to Jeff, the afternoon bartender, as he asked for a shot of whiskey to go along with the icy beer.

The bar was quiet, which allowed him to be with his thoughts. He looked around. A couple of regulars nodded to him, then went back to their conversation. Just as well; he wanted to be with his thoughts. He lit his fourth cigarette. Now, what to do about Sheila. Marry her or not? *God, tell me what to do,* he pleaded. Peter really did not believe in a higher power, but he was desperate.

He stared into his drink, watching the golden bubbles shift and change from the reflection of the overhead light. His thoughts took him back to his last relationship before Sheila.

It had started out well, as they all did, but like the rest, it ended up not working out. She started nagging him more than he cared to hear, like how he needed a better-paying job. Come to think about it, she nagged him on just about everything: sleeping too late, draining the hot water heater by taking too many long showers, cooking with too much salt, and never seeming to keep a job. None of this had been his fault, but she would not listen.

At the end of their six-year relationship, he could not take it anymore. She was not as well off as she had first said she was. She was just another liar and psycho to add to the list. He left to care for his aging mother.

After his mother died, he found that a job was hard to find when he did not really want to look for one. With the competition from the younger guys and his long absence from the workforce, he wasn't successful in even finding a part-time job. Besides, it was hard to find a job with the flexibility he needed so he would be available to go hiking, climbing, or fishing with his buddies.

Then as luck would have it, he heard that his uncle in the isolated desert of California was deteriorating and not willing to move to a city and a nursing home. Peter decided he could help this uncle, and in return, his uncle could help him. So the arrangement was made. It was not Peter's ideal setting, but it would do.

What to do? What to do? The old fart is going to die soon, and then where will I be? Peter stared down at his third drink, still not having a clear decision formed in his mind.

He focused on when he and Sheila had met. It was right here at this very spot just about two years ago. He smiled, remembering looking up when the door of the bar opened and seeing a silhouette of a shapely woman. When she moved to the interior of the bar, his breath was taken by her beauty and the confidence she displayed.

He turned on the charm and gave her a big smile. "May I buy you a drink, my lady?" he asked as he got off the barstool and bowed to her. It must have worked because they had been together ever since.

I truly am the luckiest man in the world, he thought as he returned to focusing on the golden color of the liquid-filled glass.

~~~~

I can't wait to get away from all this noise and crappy smog of LA and get to where I can see the stars, listen to the silence of the desert, and cuddle with Peter, Sheila thought as she ran through her condo by the ocean, trying to decide what to take to the cabin for the weekend.

Being with Peter was intoxicating and frustrating all at once. She loved him—she really did—but sometimes he seemed to live for himself. And sometimes his drinking got out of hand. She remembered the last time they had been together. It had been the nastiest fight they had had in their two-year relationship. They had been at a very upscale restaurant, celebrating with her coworkers after she had landed the huge new advertising contract. She knew Peter got nervous around people he did not know, but after his fourth glass of wine and two scotches, she was embarrassed by the looks her colleagues were giving each other as he loosened up more. He never got out of control, but he started out the evening hardly talking to anyone. As his body filled with booze, he started bragging about all of his accomplishments and talking too loud.

She shook her head as if to shake the horrible fight from her mind. On the drive back to her place, she had lightly mentioned that he had drunk a bit too much. She knew it did her no good to think about the fight. She hated his explosive temper, which came out of nowhere. She would rather concentrate on the beauty and brightness of his soul and that smile of his. *Yes, that feels better*, she thought.

She put a very sexy teddy in her suitcase. It was one of the few gifts Peter had given her. She pretended his lack of attention in that department did not bother her, as he so easily rocked her world in the bedroom. He was extremely attentive when he wanted to be. One evening when he stayed over, she came home from a business event, which he did not want to attend, to find candles lit throughout the condo, soft music playing in the background, and dried rose petals trailing across the floor. *Cliché but cute*, she thought as she followed the path of petals to find him lying on her bed spread-eagle with a massive hard on and a big smile on his face. She loved his surprises. With that memory making her tingle, she finished packing and headed for the door, anticipating their reunion.

Despite her tremendous success as an advertising executive, she'd not had tremendous success in relationships. Men seemed to be intimidated by her beauty, her success, and her strength. No relationship had ever lasted long, six months at the most. That was before Peter.

As Joshua trees blipped by, Sheila remembered the first time she'd seen him. She had been heading for the refuge of her wonderful cabin in the desert after yet another breakup. Pissed and frustrated, she decided to finally stop and check out the funky bar she had been passing by at ninety miles an hour in her Crossfire for years. She screeched to a halt, leaving tire marks on the pavement, whipped the car in reverse, backed up, and swung into the parking lot of the Desert Gator, creating a dust devil along the way.

She had stood in the doorway of the cool bar, allowing her eyes to adjust to the dark of the room. She made a quick scan and saw a sexy loner sitting at the end of the bar smiling at her. He took her breath away when he slid off his barstool, bowed, and asked her what she would like to drink. She was drawn to that smile, and in spite of her intuition whispering, *Don't do it,* she found a force pulling her toward this handsome stranger.

She heard herself say, "Scotch, neat." She rarely drank, but this seemed like the perfect time. After all, she had been through hell with her last relationship. She had been so in love with Jake, but he did not want a commitment. It was exactly what she did not want to hear from him, and in anger and pain, she had broken off their relationship, slammed some clothes in her bag, and headed out of town like a bat out of hell.

I will never be in a committed relationship again, she vowed. *I will never fall in love again. I never seem to pick the right guy. Relationships just don't work for me. Just do not work. Fuckin' men,* she'd thought, as she raced through the Mojave, not knowing she was heading right into her next relationship.

All this went through her head as she zipped along Interstate 15, anticipating a weekend of lovemaking. With the warm desert air filling her nostrils and playing with her hair, she dared think about what life would be like if she and Peter got married. She shivered. She did love him.

She did not like being alone, but parts of his character had started to bother her more. Shortly into their relationship, she began to notice that Peter only thought of Peter. Peter did things for her only if it benefited him. But the things he did for her, she enjoyed. Coming home to a clean house and home-cooked meal with good conversation was something she had longed for and had found unexpectedly in Peter. That was just one of the things that kept her hanging on. But his excessive drinking and explosive temper scared her, and she increasingly found herself monitoring her words and actions when around him. She was starting to get exhausted from it.

The disturbing thoughts pushed up from deep in the dark recesses of her mind. She did not want to think about them for fear that, if she did, she would have to make a decision: stay with him or break up. And she did not want to go to that place in her mind.

She pressed on the accelerator, speeding toward her destination. Sheila yelled to the dust devil far to her left, as it raced across a dry lakebed toward the horizon, "Besides, at this point in my life, something is better than nothing!" She cranked the music up louder, preferring to get lost in the blaring sound as it drowned out her disturbing thoughts.

An hour later, Sheila whipped into the circle drive in front of her lavish cabin overlooking a beautiful, plant-filled desert, outlined with pinto-brown mountains. This was her refuge. This was where her soul refueled and rested. She turned on the hot tub before going into the house to unpack. Looking at the clock hanging on the wall in the well-stocked, spacious kitchen, she saw that she had plenty of time before Peter arrived. *I have time for a long run followed by a hot soak before Peter shows up.* Excited to have the place all to herself for a bit, she hurried and dressed for her run.

She decided to run along the main road toward the Desert Gator and look for Peter coming. The thought of being with him excited her deep within her soul, as long as she did not think about his stinginess and his temper tantrums. As she ran, she debated his good and bad points and kept coming back to the same conclusion. She decided it was better to be with him than to be alone. Part of her decision was based on the fact she was not getting any younger. Being almost fifty two, she would one day lose her attractiveness, as she had started to notice, and she would need someone to take care of her.

She realized that if they did marry, she would have to be the breadwinner. Could she live with that? As her toned legs guided her feet along the edge of the road and her breathing started to find its rhythm, she decided that she could indeed live with the fact that he was lazy when it came to working. The payoff, she decided, was worth it. She would come home to a clean house, dinner being cooked, and most importantly, someone who loved her. Truly, what human could ask for more? As she ran with her back to the setting sun and toward the distant purple mountains, she made a decision to test the waters over the weekend to see how he felt about marriage.

Content, Sheila ran east toward her destiny. As she ran, she filled her lungs with the cooling air of the magical early evening desert, filling her soul with unconditional love for a flawed man.

~~~~

Yes, Peter thought, as he drained the last drop of alcohol from his mug, *I will ask her to marry me tonight. I will watch what I drink this weekend and be on my best behavior, and I will turn on the Anderson charm. Sheila will not be able to turn me down.* Luckily for him, he even had a wedding ring: his mother's.

Full of confidence, Peter waved goodbye to Clyde the bar owner and headed out the door. He tripped over his feet heading to his truck and dropped his keys in the dirt. Cussing, he almost fell over picking up the set of keys. *Gotta watch my drinking. No more tonight*, he thought as he climbed into the cab of the truck and again fumbled with putting the key in the ignition, which only made him explode with unstable anger. *Oops, gotta watch that too*, he thought.

Peter headed west toward the setting sun and his future. Lighting his last cigarette, he cranked up the hard rock music. Blasting the base, he took a deep drag on the fresh nicotine and allowed it to assist the beer and whiskey in settling his nerves. *Must think positive.*

Way in the distance against the backdrop of the purple, pink, and coral desert mountains and the bright light of the setting sun, he could see a figure off to the side of the road. His heart raced. His meal ticket was jogging. He would throw her a kiss as he passed by her and get to the cabin, where he would have a delicious meal started for them, a romantic table set with candles, and an open bottle of wine before she got back.

Peter grinned at the thought, pushed a bit harder on the gas pedal, and pounded his hands on the steering wheel to the beat of the drums blasting from the four speakers in the truck.

Forgetting he had his last cigarette in his hand, he dropped it between his legs. It burned his calf as it fell, and the pain made him cry out. Frantically looking for the butt, he took his eyes off the road and focused on the chore at hand. Within seconds, he heard the wheels leave the pavement and felt a horrible thump. Jamming on the brakes, he jumped out of the truck and swept the cigarette out of the floor of the cab before it could catch the carpet on fire. Then he remembered the thud he had heard.

At the back of his truck, he saw the most horrific sight: a pretzel-twisted body.

"Sheila, Sheila, Sheila," he cried as he ran to her side.

Her dead eyes were wide open in surprise. Off in the distance, the coyotes cowered as they heard the high rumbling of a bloodcurdling scream come from the road.

"Oh, my God, what the hell were you doing running in the middle of the road," he screamed at her, as he shook her to bring life back into her broken, dead body. "Why in the hell were you running in the road?" No sound came from the love of his life.

He looked up from the lifeless body he was holding and realized with fright that they were not in the road but ten yards to the side of it. While looking for his lit cigarette, he had driven his truck right off the road and into his sugar mama.

Cradling her in his arms, stroking her hair, and hysterically sobbing, he rocked them both back and forth. "Why do bad things always happen to me?" he yelled to the silent space around them. "Why?"

Then slowly it dawned on him: he was going to jail. No getting out of this one. He had no relative or sympathetic friend to bail him out. He was done. It was over. No amount of charm could save him now. His ass was grass, and he was fried.

Busted.

Then from the depth of his being, a tiny spark of a new thought began to form. He would be taken care of. Not in the way he would have liked. But at least he would have a roof over his head and three meals a day. *I guess I will have to get used to being someone's bitch,* Peter thought with sadness, as he rocked back and forth waiting for someone to drive by.

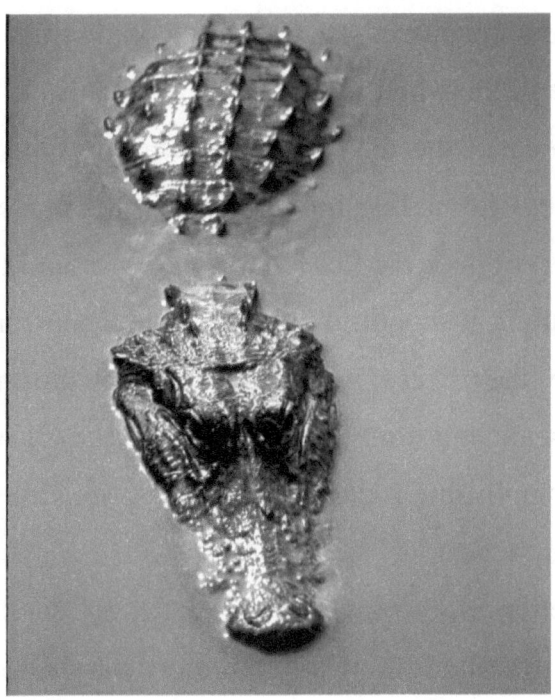

Chapter 6

Desert Gator

The sloping desert floor flowed out endlessly in all directions, stopping at the base of colorful desert mountains without a person or animal in sight. Only one lone building sat in the middle of the widest part of the desert valley floor. In stark contrast to the hues of browns and purples, it was painted a bright turquoise on one side, orange on another, green on the third, and deep purple on the last side. The flat roof was white and red painted in a checkerboard pattern.

Not even a passed-out drunk could miss seeing it, especially at night when car lights reflected back psychedelic colors not seen in the daylight. That was the intention of the owner, Clyde, who had designed and built the place as a much-needed watering hole for the local desert rats and tourists who drove by in their air-conditioned cars to other destinations. And just in case they were not thirsty in this inferno, he had purchased an ancient toothless alligator named Ol' Gate from a bankrupted small-time traveling circus and set him up out back as a tourist attraction.

What better way to make a living for an alcoholic than to own a bar in the middle of an extremely parched desert? And he did make money. Clyde was set.

He had come from Australia to America over thirty years ago to start his life over after losing his beautiful wife and soul mate, Patty, to a long and painful illness. To make it even more painful, he not only lost her, he also lost his baby she was carrying. The pain for him was more than the vastness of Australia could contain. So he left the continent, drinking to numbness as he wandered the remote places of the planet for years. Along the way on his journeys, he had picked up unique cooking skills that served him well.

Finally, he settled down on this little patch of rock in the middle of the American Southwest, far from the nearest town, where he would hardly be exposed to people talking about their families, wives, and kids. He wanted none of that, for it reminded him of what he'd lost.

He had found a place where recluses thrived, a no-man's-land. Only one road cut through the isolated heart of this part of the desert, a no-shoulder, two-lane road laid out on the contours of the land. Without culverts or drainage ditches to redirect the flash floods that occasionally happened, that road had been constructed and maintained as cheaply as possible. Following the hills, the road flowed east to west, stretching from one horizon to another, eventually ending up nowhere. If one was not focused while driving on this roller coaster of asphalt, one could easily become vulture food very quickly.

This suited him just fine. He had to make a living somehow, and it did not take him long to realized that even reclusive desert rats needed a good watering hole to wet their throats and drive their pathetic memories deeper into the recesses of their minds.

So he set about building the most beautiful, tacky bar. There would be no mistake of the place not being seen. The clashing colors had a magical pull on the people driving by, so that curiosity eventually got the best of them. Once inside, seeing all the eclectic junk on the walls, meeting the happy-go-lucky chubby owner, and tasting food from the cleverly written menu, they were hooked.

Spiced Road Kill Buffalo Burger with caramelized onions

and sautéed mushrooms was the favorite of the tourists, along with at least one 16-ounce icy beer to wash it down. His homemade Prickly Pear Peach Pie was known far and wide as the best dessert in the desert. Top that off with a sixteen-year-old scotch, and there was nothing better in the outback of the great American Southwest.

The inside of the building was dark and cool, and for a moment in time, rats and tourists alike could get a reprieve from the blistering heat of the unforgiving desert. The atmosphere of the Desert Gator was like a garage sale gone very wrong. Besides the snow sled and full-sized overstuffed moose hanging from the ceiling, the walls were decorated with several jackalope heads, a dried cactus wrapped in colorful outdoor Christmas lights, buffalo robes, and one big butt of an elk on the wall, which substituted at times for a dartboard.

The local patrons were just as colorful. There was Rita, along with her companion, Bill, who lived out to the north about fifteen miles. She could barely see, and he could barely hear, but they made a harmonious pair when they were not fighting. Like clockwork, they always came in on Thursdays when Bill received his pension.

Then there was Peter, the talkative braggart. Clyde put up with him, for he made himself useful by helping bartend on short notice, changing out the kegs, and being a gofer for Clyde when he could not get away from the bar, picking up much needed supplies from the nearby town thirty miles away. That was why he did not mind too much carrying Peter on credit for his libations. Clyde considered it one of the costs of doing business.

Jake was the loner of all the loners. No one could remember the last time he spoke to anyone. He would come into the bar dressed in greasy overalls, nod to the nearest person, make his way to sit in the farthest, darkest corner, and drink his meal, only to leave with a nod as he headed out the door. No one knew exactly where he lived or what he did for a living. Rumor had it that he mined gold in the nearby hills. But it was just rumor.

Sally—now Clyde looked forward to her monthly visits. An elementary schoolteacher, she would stay in one of the less cluttered back rooms of the bar on her way to hike one of the many washes the desert had to offer. They would sit out back with Ol' Gate and chat after Clyde closed the bar. She reminded him of his long-gone Patty.

Over the years, Clyde came to view the local barflies as his kids, and little by little, the pain in his heart lessened. He knew each person's preferred drink and usually had it waiting for them before they sat down. They appreciated it, feeling special. He even got to know some of the more frequent tourists, who stopped by to dry out their bodies from the heat of the road and wash down the dust in their throats.

He especially looked forward to the Robinson family, who always stopped in on their way from the coast to visit ancient parents in the town nearest the bar. Most of the time they had their now ten-year-old twins with them, Gabriel and Moses, who loved to feed and pet Ol' Gate. The kids would help clean out his pond and pen, which Clyde appreciated, as he was starting to slow down. The hard traveling years were starting to catch up with him.

Lately he had been waking up from a sound sleep, screaming from acute pain in his stomach, a cold sweat across his body. His last checkup at the doctor's in San Bernardino showed nothing was wrong. For a time the pain disappeared, but recently it came back.

Work became tedious, and his lack of laughter coming from the big commercial kitchen did not go unnoticed by those who made the Desert Gator their second home. The change in him was reflected in the slow detrition of the bar and the thick accumulating dust on the wall hangings. But the desert rats didn't mind. They were used to the desert eventually claiming everything in it, including them.

After Clyde closed the bar, it was his custom to sit out back with Ol' Gate, telling the creature about his day, as he fed the toothless gator from the bucket of kitchen scraps.

Clyde drank his sixth of the usual eight beers for the evening, while the sun slowly laid a purple blanket over the mountains to the west. He never tired of the changing colors the evening sky had to offer. He stayed out late under the desert night sky, watching the desert blanket turn from purple to black and waiting for the stars to turn on their full brightness. In the early morning shadows, he stiffly pried himself out of the faded lawn chair and slowly made his way to his room in the back of the bar to pass out.

~~~

Clyde watched the last of the patrons leave, a group of rowdy, uppity Hollywood types who acted like they owned the place. This group never tipped when they dropped in, but at least they paid for the barrels of booze and big orders of food they consumed. Clyde could live with that.

He had let the bartender/waitress leave hours ago when he realized this group once again was settling in to make a late night of partying in the Desert Gator before heading on back to LA. He did not want to subject his "kids" to prolonged rants about who was the best director in the film industry, debates about whether black and whites would make a comeback, and blah-blah-blah.

Wiping down the bar counter for the last time, he took a big bottle of Celtic Knot from the shelf, took it out back, and placed it next to his faded lawn chair and the pistol. He picked up a full can of kerosene and went back inside.

Taking his time, he splashed it on the walls, the sled, the big old buffalo head with a stick of dynamite protruding out of its mouth like a fat Cuban cigar, and don't forget the elk's butt. He doused an extra splash of kerosene on the ol' gal. Looking around and feeling satisfied that he had soaked just about everything in sight, he set the can down and joined Ol' Gate out back one last time.

Ol' Gate waited patiently for the bucket of kitchen scraps that would not come this time. Clyde sat for a long time taking in the vast horizon. He thought of his life, how he had wanted it to be, but fate and roads had taken him in a different direction. He had come to this place a broken, lost man, but through the people and the healing spirit of the desert, he had come to love his life in this hole.

And it was for that very reason he decided he could not burden himself on any of those he loved. He had watched his wife die of a slow and painful illness, and he did not want those he had come to love to witness his.

With his plan in place, he drained most of the last half of the hundred-proof whiskey, leaving just enough in the bottom for good measure, stuffed the bottle with a whiskey-soaked cloth, lit the end sticking out, and tossed it into the open door to the back of the bar. He watched the flames catch quickly on the dry, bleached wood.

He sat his chunky body down next to Ol' Gate, picked up

the gun, and put a bullet in his head just as the flames reached every stick of dynamite in every nook and cranny of the place, and blew it into toothpicks.

When the dust settled, in place where the bar used to sit, was now a big deep pond created by the blast, which had disturbed an underground aquifer. Clear, cool fresh water came bubbling up to the surface, creating a large, deep pond in the middle of the desert.

People from miles around heard the blast and felt the earth shake, and many saw the cloud of smoke over the site of the Desert Gator. By the time the people had made their way across the desert to where the Desert Gator had been, Ol' Gate had consumed Clyde whole. He sauntered to his new expanded home and slid effortlessly into the cool water to digest his meal, a generous gift from his friend. There he lived out his days, feasting on the unfortunate birds and occasional animals that made a pit stop at the Desert Gator.

Chapter 7

A New Beginning

A quarter of a century old, and what do I have to show for it? Wendy pondered as she lay on the couch, looking out the living room window at the top of the pine trees swaying gently in the breeze.

As the tree tops moved from side to side, carrying her to her past, she remembered when she first met him. It was early spring. Soon she would graduate from high school, and that had terrified her to her core. Moving out on her own, living away from home, scared her to death. Her exterior was tough, confident, and bubbly. No one could have guessed how ineffective, inadequate, unimportant, and afraid she felt. Inside she trembled at the thought of what came after graduation, and it kept her up late into the night with worry.

So as she paid for her coffee at the quaint deli near the school, she felt eyes upon her. Looking around the room, her eyes landed on a handsome young man sitting at a small table in the back corner of the store. She found herself intrigued by his long blond hair and deep green eyes. When their eyes met, he smiled at her, and for the first time in a long time, she did not feel so alone. She smiled back as she left the deli to meet up with some friends.

Unable to shake the brief encounter with the mysterious college boy, she found herself returning to the deli more in hopes of running into him again. Finally, a few weeks later, she did, and thus began her nightmare life with Jacob, though in the beginning it was absolute bliss.

Never having dated during high school or ever having a boyfriend, Jacob was godsent. He told her all the things she had imagined a boyfriend would tell her: how beautiful she was, how he loved her long black hair, and the way she made him feel when they made love. For the first time in a long time, she felt wanted, valued, needed, and loved. So when he asked her to marry him, she did not hesitate. Finally, someone wanted her. She would not be alone, and she would be so very happy.

Yet deep in her core, tucked in the folds of her being, she knew she was making a huge mistake. But the crippling fear of being by herself overpowered the thought. The fear helped her keep that knowledge beyond her conscious mind. She had no choice.

At nineteen years old, she found herself a happily married woman and living in married housing on the campus of Michigan State University while her husband pursued a degree in forestry biology and she in home economics. But soon that happiness would turn into incredible sadness, creating a shell of existence.

Slowly over time, Jacob became insecure and controlling. He went from accidently opening her mail and occasionally waiting for her outside the door of her classes to opening all her mail and walking her to all her classes and being there when they let out to escort her home. Eventually he started asking her each and every time when any male of any age passed within their vicinity how cute he was on a scale of 1-10 compared to him. It became so bad that she kept her head down whenever they were in public or driving in the car. She found herself doing anything and everything to avoid an argument. Their arguments were becoming more and more frequent, to the point where a neighbor yelled at her one afternoon that if she did not quit screaming, he would call the police on her. This made her feel even more isolated. She couldn't reach out to anyone. No trust.

She began to realize Jacob was insane, and life was not

going to get better. Yet through it all, she would tell herself she did not want to be a divorced woman, just another statistic. The marriage would improve only if she tried harder. She had no choice.

But sometimes she would get so frustrated and angry. When she stood up to him, she faced even harsher arguments, fights, and eventually physical abuse. One time he hit her so hard with a cupped hand that her eardrum perforated from the force of his swing. For what seemed like days, she lay on the couch with a towel under her head as her ear bled. As she healed, she listened to him apologize over and over, crying that it would never happen again if only she didn't look at other men. She tried harder after that to be a better wife, while slowly drying up and dying inside.

Eventually they graduated and headed off to a new life where Jacob would work for the Forest Service. Her hopes were high, and she thought this new life would bring a change in him for the better. Maybe with a good-paying job in the field he loved, he would be happier and therefore treat her better. He might stop calling her names, belittling her at every turn, and laughing at her to make himself feel better.

She could only wish, for the fear of living alone was still too strong in her for her to act. What she really wanted to do was to run. But to where? And how? So she stayed and endured, as she had no other choice.

For a short while, things did get better, but then they became unbearable. Because they lived in semi-isolation, their arguments were only heard by the animals of the forest and the birds of the trees. When need be, she became an excellent liar, making up incredible yet believable stories of how she got the bruises on her arms or the occasional black eye or the broken wrist. Since they moved each season, they were never in one place long enough for people to connect the dots, so the lies were easy to invent. No one really knew the two of them.

He did not physically hurt her often, but the constant verbal abuse was more than she could take at times. When she would lash out, however, she endured physical pain at his hands. She actually preferred the physical pain, for it was easier to deal with than the emotional pain. That pain eventually planted itself and grew in her psyche. She no longer needed him around to tell her how worthless she was, how clumsy and stupid. She now was telling herself that without his help.

Three years into their marriage, he started accusing her of having affairs. But how could she, even if she had wanted to, which she didn't? She never went anywhere unless he was with her. Where was he getting these stupid ideas? She knew she had not done anything to cause these accusations. In fact, she started to notice that these accusations of her being with other men only happened when he stayed late at work with consuming projects. Then it dawned on her—he was having an affair and transferring his guilt or whatever onto her. How much more could she take?

But the fear of being alone was still more frightening than the life she was living. She was stuck. She had no choice.

Lying beside him after having sex, for it had long since stopped being love, and long after he had gone to sleep, she would rehearse over and over in her mind just exactly how she would leave him. She would then imagine her life being happy and fulfilling, with numerous friends and a job she loved and a place of her own decorated just the way she wanted. Each and every night for the last year, this was her process before she finally succumbed to sleep.

As time went on, her days were spent in a daze, with her barely existing or noticing life around her. The light from the moon and stars or the sound of quail scurrying by went unnoticed. She was slowly dying from the inside out, and there was nothing she could do about it. It was only her nightly thoughts that kept her alive. She rehearsed escape, playing it over and over in her mind, as she fell asleep next to the monster.

On her twenty-fifth birthday, lying on the couch, mesmerized by the gentle sway of the trees, she realized she was a quarter of a century old. She felt ancient. Where would she be in another quarter of a century when she was fifty? Would she be in the same place or dead?

She allowed the trees to lull her, and four hours went by within seconds. She had not fallen asleep. She had not moved off the couch, yet four hours had vanished. This truly frightened her. Where had she gone? She had no frickin' idea. Inside she felt completely empty. Alone. Lost. She was a shell. There was just an ever-so-tiny flicker of light burning ever so low. There was nothing left inside of her. The light was almost gone. Nothing left. It was all gone. What was happening to her? She felt she was losing herself to a void, falling deeper into a never-ending hole of nonexistence.

Then at the core of her soul, tucked in the folds of her being, where long ago she had placed herself for safekeeping, a thought began to take form and surface like a hot-air balloon rising from the ground to the heights of the sky. As the thought began to take form, it began to merge into her conscious mind. Once fully and solidly formed, it shook her to her core. It screamed at her, *Having no choice is a choice. By staying where you are and making no choice, you have made your choice.*

She sat up, fully cognizant for the first time in her life that her destiny was in her hands. She had a choice not to live this way if she so chose. By doing nothing, she had chosen to stay where she was. It was liberating and frightening all at once. But she had never felt more hopeful or alive as she did in that very moment. She could do something about her situation, make a different choice, but what was she to do?

The nightly plan she had rehearsed surfaced quickly, as if it had been waiting in the dungeon of darkness for eons for the light to rescue it and draw it up to the surface of her mind. She would wait till next month. Between jobs, they would be back in the town where it all began, visiting family. With the strength of being with her own family, she would leave him. Leave him! For the first time in years, she breathed in a deep, expansive breath and felt so alive and hopeful.

~~~~

It was 4:00 a.m., time to leave. She had not slept all night, having decided the day before that this was the day to leave. She could wait no longer. Waiting any longer would pull her back into the depths of hell from which there would be no escape. She would truly die.

Having argued with him all the way across the country, she told him in the living room of her parents' home with them standing by as witnesses that she needed to take a break. Much to her surprise, he agreed.

Racing down Route 66 at eighty miles per hour in her Datsun B210, heading far away from purgatory, she went into survival mode. Watching the road in her headlights, she thought about her life: where she had come from and where she was going. All her possessions in her car, knowing she could only go forward for there was nothing left behind her, she did her best not to be so afraid and pressed harder on the gas pedal. She remembered she had finally made a choice.

Driving toward the east, in the middle of the shoulder-less lonely desert road, she passed the ancient crater and later whizzed by the tackiest, brightest, most colorful waterhole. Shooting past a popular rock-climbing site near a long, dry riverbed, she passed an isolated, seldom-used hiking trail to one of the best viewing sites for the Milky Way. She pressed on.

Fear gripped her, but she could not go back. She would not go back. The past would kill her. The unknown future frightened her but not as much as staying mired in her past. For the first time since a child, she prayed.

Funny, in all the years of being in an empty, abusive marriage, she never prayed or even thought of praying, but here in the middle of the beautiful stretched-out desert, heading into the unknown, she prayed. She spoke aloud to whatever higher power there was, vowing that no matter what was out there in the future, she would be okay. She would survive. She would make it. But the fear was still in her solar plexus.

Deep in thought, she did not realize the world around her was changing, getting lighter. She continued to let go and let God, little by little. "Let go. Let God. Let go. Let God," she repeated to herself, over and over. She surrendered for the first time in her life to a power stronger, wiser, and older than the universe.

And just as she let go, surrendered, feeling the tight ball that had forever been in her gut loosen, the sun fully crested the mountain on the horizon to her right front, running across the stark desert floor, and shot glowing hot new morning rays of sunlight into her car that penetrated her very soul.

Wendy felt a fulfilling, calming sense of peace, and a deep, clear, crisp knowing that she wouldn't just be okay, she would thrive. No matter what was out there, what she might encounter in her future, she would be okay. She was not alone. And as the sun continued to fill her with healing light, she smiled a deep, knowing smile and pressed on, driving the road to her soul into her future of a new beginning.

Over the years and events of her life, she had traveled many roads: smooth ones, dead-end ones, ones with no warning of a sharp curve ahead, others with deep drop-offs, mountainous winding roads, flat wide roads and ones with breathtaking vistas. None ever had a more profound effect on her than that first lonely desert road she drove.

~~~~

Decades later, she would find herself traveling this very same road again. She was enjoying driving in the dark, moonless night on the two-lane highway to nowhere, her thoughts traveling back in time, reliving her life, when it happened. The road suddenly disappeared between mile marker 165 and 164.

About the Author

Carmen Mendoza is a credentialed certified business/life coach with international clientele. She received her Master's degree in Education from Colorado State University and worked there for 10 years with Extension and 4-H.

Her background is eclectic. At sixteen, she worked for the Parks and Recreation Department of 29 Palms, California, where she also went to high school. Over her lifetime, she worked for the Bureau of Indian Affairs, the National Park Service, in radio advertising, as a secondary school teacher, and as director of a youth drug prevention program. She is currently living in northern Colorado and is involved with various cultural and community groups; Colorado Tartan Day Council, Clan MacKay Society, Museo de los Tres Colonies, Elks, Zonta and Colorado Women of Influence. Continuing with her eclecticism, she is now venturing into writing.

For more information on Carmen, visit **www.carmendoza.com**.

www.ingramcontent.com/pod-product-compliance
Lightning Source LLC
Chambersburg PA
CBHW030233180626
46810CB00008B/3108